"_____ e."

Ruby turn_____ s cold skin, she whispered against his scratchy cheek, ignoring the slight softening inside her at the utter maleness swirling around her in a he_____ ne tried to lift her arms _____ n.

"God help me," _____

Fresh panic flare_____ f response. His pain, the agony of his hunger, threatened to consume her . . . but this emotion, his desire, made her purr and arch against him.

He nudged Ruby higher and released one of her arms. Instead of shoving at him with her hand, she curled her fingers into a naked shoulder, hissing at the contact, at the sensation of smooth male flesh . . . instantly infused with all his need, all his dark *wanting*. For her.

Her mouth opened wide against his bristly cheek. A sharp cry ripped from her throat.

God help her, as his desire rose, the blackness receded, faded to nothing.

"Sebastian," he spat out, his cheek rippling against lips as he spoke.

"What?" She felt drunk, addled in the head.

"My name . . . is Sebastian."

"Heated passion, fast-paced action, and a world of werewolves you never knew existed."
—Bestselling author Robin

ALSO BY SHARIE KOHLER

Marked by Moonlight
Kiss of a Dark Moon

TO CRAVE A
BLOOD MOON

SHARIE KOHLER

Pocket Books

New York   London   Toronto   Sydney

Pocket Books
A Division of Simon & Schuster, Inc.
1230 Avenue of the Americas
New York, NY 10020

This book is a work of fiction. Names, characters, places, and incidents either are products of the author's imagination or are used fictitiously. Any resemblance to actual events or locales or persons, living or dead, is entirely coincidental.

First Pocket Books paperback edition September 2009

POCKET and colophon are registered trademarks of Simon & Schuster, Inc.

For information about special discounts for bulk purchases, please contact Simon & Schuster Special Sales at 1-866-506-1949 or business@simonandschuster.com.

The Simon & Schuster Speakers Bureau can bring authors to your live event. For more information or to book an event contact the Simon & Schuster Speakers Bureau at 1-866-248-3049 or visit our website at www.simonspeakers.com.

Cover art by Chris Cocozza. Cover design by Min Choi.

Manufactured in the United States of America

10 9 8 7 6 5 4 3 2 1

ISBN 978-1-4391-0158-2
ISBN 978-1-4391-2700-1 (ebook)

For my talented, wonderful friend,
Tera Lynn Childs— who just plain gets me.
And loves me anyway.

TO CRAVE A
BLOOD MOON

Prologue

The slam of the screen door cracked on the night. Ruby crawled from bed, dropping to her feet and sliding into her waiting slippers. Light glowed softly through the open door of her room. Voices rolled on the air.

Angry. Mad.

Her tummy cramped. Whimpering, she hugged the wall and peered out the door, bringing her stuffed duck to her mouth to gnaw.

"Richard," she heard Mommy say. "Please. Don't go."

The screen door creaked as it always did when someone stood in the threshold, holding it open.

"You made your choice," he snapped. "Now I'm making mine."

Something that felt very close to hate rolled off him, finding Ruby where she huddled. She bit down on her duck's floppy bill. Her stomach cramped tighter, twisting, and she felt her dinner of peas, potatoes and meatloaf rise up in her throat.

"For God's sake, Richard. What choice is there? She's our daughter—"

"No, she's weird, Diane. She's a weird kid. And I can't stand to be around her. My own goddamned daughter!"

Tears burned her eyes. Ruby buried her nose in her stuffed duck and fought the urge to suck her thumb. Big girls didn't suck their thumbs.

"If you won't listen to me, listen to your mother," Daddy continued in that ugly voice that made her cringe. "Your sister. Even your own family thinks she's—"

"Stop it. Enough." Mommy's voice dropped to a quick hush. "You're right."

Closing her eyes, Ruby muttered a silent, fervent prayer, begging Jesus to make Daddy love her. Make her the kind of little girl a daddy could love.

The screen door groaned. Someone was pulling it wider. "You've made your choice," Mommy said. "Now I'm making mine. Get out."

The door slammed, the sound reverberating on the night, making her jump. Her duck fell. She edged back from the door, her heart seizing in her chest, hurting, hurting. The hurt was so bad she couldn't even breathe.

Daddy was gone.

Because of her.

Mommy's footsteps started toward her room. Ruby flew back into her bed and pulled the covers to her chin, pretending to be asleep.

A moment later, she felt the bed sink with her mother's weight. Mommy folded her discarded duck into her arms and curled her body around her.

"Mommy?" she asked, eyes still jammed shut.

Her mother's chest rumbled against her back. "Go to sleep, baby."

"Is Daddy—"

"It's late. We'll talk tomorrow." Pause. "We're going to be fine, baby girl. Happy," her mother said, in the voice she used when trying to convince Ruby that black-eyed peas tasted good. Just like regular peas.

She knew the voice. Knew that Mommy was pretending now. But then Ruby knew. She always knew.

"It's okay, baby girl. We're going to be fine." She rocked her now, her hand smoothing over her hair.

The tight embrace only made Ruby *feel* more, made Mommy's pain wash over her in burning waves. *Desolation. Regret.*

All of Mommy's hurt bled into her. Hot sobs rose in the back of her throat, but Ruby held them back, kept them stuffed inside so Mommy wouldn't know that Daddy was right. *She was weird*. Only someone weird could feel what other people were feeling.

A sound must have escaped her.

Mommy stroked the side of her face.

"Hush, baby. I can't stand it when you hurt."

Ruby didn't have the heart to tell her it was *her* pain that made her hurt. Mommy hugged her tighter, and Ruby fought back a scream. Biting her lip, the coppery tang of blood ran over her teeth. But she didn't utter a complaint. Complaints were what drove Daddy away. And kept anyone from wanting to be her friend at school.

From now on, she would never complain again. She would never tell. Then she wouldn't scare anyone.

And Mommy wouldn't leave her, too.

1

He had moved beyond the point of pain.

Weeks had passed since Sebastian Santiago felt anything except bone-deep numbness. His carefully constructed shields remained in place while his beast prowled, hidden inside him. For now, it would wait in that dark, secret part of himself. And endure.

All to survive. To protect Rafe. He couldn't lead his brother here, to this place. To these soulless bastards. He couldn't let them know that he wasn't alone. That others like him existed.

Bending his head at an odd angle against the moldy stone at his back, he watched the female beside him drag a blood-red nail across his chest. With moonrise so close, Annika was exceptionally vicious today. Not that she had ever been a cupcake with him. She had declared him her special pet the first day he arrived. Her nail increased its pressure, breaking skin as she drew a jagged line through his flesh. His chest surged against her hand, but he held silent as blood welled up, more black than red in the darkened cell.

Water dripped somewhere, a monotonous, lonely sound. He counted each drip, letting it occupy his thoughts. *Ping. Ping. Ping.* His tongue salivated, yearning to find the source and press his parched lips to it. They'd fed him this morning, but hadn't bothered to supply water. Maybe they would remember tomorrow.

The ancient ground pulsed beneath him, cold with fallen blood. His. And the others that came before. Every full moon his captors gorged themselves. And blood ran. Swam down the walls. A corrugated river through the old building's bones. He smelled it still. Could taste it in the air.

He inhaled harder, past wood, rock and mortar, past the taint of blood. A distant whiff of the world outside teased his nose, calling to him. Freedom— where the air smelled fresh, wet from the rain he had heard last night and the wash of sea at the city's every side.

He closed his eyes, imagining he was out there.

Instead of a dozen feet below earth where his nights and days were consumed in dark torment.

His eyes adjusted to the blackness with ease, seeing the movements and faces around him. A second female sidled near. An animal slinking closer. The coppery tang of blood seeped from her every pore. She pulled her dress over her head, revealing her sleek body. *Catriona*, he thought her name. *Remember their names. Know each and every one so you can kill them later.* He never once questioned his survival. He was a hard man to kill. *Man.* His lips curved cruelly, a harsh breath of laughter escaping him.

Annika frowned and dug her hand into his face, forcing his attention back on her. Greedy bitch. Her talon-like fingers delved through the bristly growth of beard. The smell of his own blood on her hand filled his nose.

She spoke to him in her tongue. He spoke several languages, but his Turkish was rusty. Even so, it had improved vastly since his imprisonment. "What is wrong, my pet?" she demanded in her guttural voice. "Our games amuse you?"

Their hands slithered like serpents on his body. Catriona bent over his chest and lapped up his blood with the rough rasp of her tongue. As if the taste of him was too much, she groaned and bit down. He surged against the force of her bite, eyes squeezing shut as the bitch made a snack of him with her blunt little teeth.

Annika shoved Catriona aside and bent to taste from where she had carved her mark on his chest. Catriona took exception and slapped her. Annika came up hissing fury, and the other female backed down, dipping those eerie pewter eyes. A strict code of hierarchy existed within packs. Clearly Annika held more rank.

Annika returned to him.

He forced himself away, floating outside himself, watching like a spectator as the two bitches played with him, a mouse in their paws. As they had done for months now.

Two moonrises had passed since they captured him off the streets. Two moonrises he had endured all manner of depravities. They enjoyed his resilience, their freedom to torture him again and again.

Annika's hand gripped his cock, her touch soft and coaxing, directly opposite from the savagery that edged her features.

The only time they ever treated him to gentleness was when they wanted to rouse him. Physically, he could not prevent himself from responding. His body had become his worst enemy—his greatest weakness. No matter how he loathed them, they succeeded in using him.

The scrape of hinges filled the air momentarily, saving him from the females' appetites. A warm blast of air swept into the frigid cell, accompanied by light. The suddenness of it stung his eyes. He held a hand over his face, squinting to see who his newest tormentor would be.

Gunter stood there. The pack alpha had made only two appearances since Sebastian's capture. Once at the beginning of his captivity, and another a month ago . . . to check on his progress.

With a snap of his fingers, the two females left Sebastian's side, their heads dipped in deference to the pack's master. With lingering glances full of dark promise, they left him alone with the alpha.

Gunter entered the cell, his well-tailored linen slacks and white shirt a stark contrast to the dungeon that had become Sebastian's world.

Standing over Sebastian, he grimaced at the sight of his soiled and naked body, shaking his head. "You look like shit."

Sebastian levered himself up on his elbows. The chains rattled, the manacles at his ankles and wrists pulling, digging into bone. His skin had long rubbed free. Raw muscle and sinew hung in torn tatters. Until free of the manacles, his body could not regenerate.

"Your hospitality has lacked somewhat."

"Indeed?" The alpha cocked his head to the side, amusement lacing his voice. "Any number of men would be glad for the attention you've been given. Fucked daily by beautiful women. What complaint can you possibly have?"

Sebastian's lip curled. "Is that what you call them? Women? I think sewer rats a more apt description."

Gunter tossed back his head with a laugh. After a moment, he sobered, his silver eyes a steady molten stream. "All for naught, it would seem. None of them are breeding. It appears we are not a compatible species, after all. Shame."

Sebastian tensed, both relieved and alarmed. Since he never made it a habit to sleep with lycans, he had not known if he could impregnate any of the females who had used him for stud in the last weeks.

Gunter continued, "Unfortunate, I know. I cannot breed your special talents into my pack. So what shall I do with you?" He cocked his head in contemplation, tapping his lip. The room's shadows cast menacing lights to his features.

"I've an idea," Sebastian murmured, lifting one manacled wrist to his propped knee as if he were not chained to a wall in a dungeon. "You can let me go."

Gunter tsked. "So you can continue picking off my kind at your leisure? I have enough to worry about as it is without setting some hybrid loose who fancies himself the annihilator of my race."

Sebastian shrugged, trying to appear unaffected as he lied, "Who says I have to continue my ways?" Hunting his distant brethren was what Sebastian did best. Until now, until he'd been captured, he'd excelled at it. He would never stop.

"No. Can't have you running about," he continued as if Sebastian hadn't spoken. "I've other problems. We're at war with a particularly bothersome cell of lycans on the rise in the west."

There'd always been feuding between packs. A territorial species, they could never come to an accord, which was man's greatest defense against them. "You mean I might be lucky enough and you might kill each other off."

Gunter's eyes glittered an unholy silver. "I had hoped you would be a useful weapon. And you may yet."

Unease crawled through his chest, cracking at his armor of numbness, just a fissure, but the first crack nonetheless. "How is that?"

"I need merely convince you to join our side."

Sebastian snorted. "That will never happen." He possessed a soul. Nothing would change that . . . change him into a demon that glutted himself every moonrise and sank deeper and deeper into damnation. He wasn't damned. No matter that his mother spent her life reminding him that at his core he was Satan's spawn.

"Oh, it will happen." Gunter strode several feet and lifted Sebastian's breakfast tray from where Annika had kicked it in her haste to have him this morning. Before the day's depravities began, he had licked his bowl of oatmeal clean, desperate for the nourishment. "You might just be a half-breed dog, but the half of you that's like me will guarantee it will happen." He rolled a finger against the inside of his bowl, then tasted. "Hmm. Honey. Sweet. But your next meal will be even sweeter—of the human variety."

Blood rushed to Sebastian's head, and he grasped at his roiling emotions, desperate to keep them in check, buried deep where they could not be detected by his brother a world away. He'd lasted this long, he could hang on longer. He had to.

"Never fear, I shall make certain it's something delectable. Female, of course. And young. The freshest is always young."

He surged against his chains, the steel striking his wrist bones with a clang that should have been agony . . . but only paled beside the horror of the alpha's words. "You bastard—"

Laughing, Gunter strode from the cell. The heavy

door clanged shut after him, the bolt sliding home the final sound in the charged silence.

Sebastian dropped his head to his bare knees, his fingers digging cruelly into his flesh. His heart raced. Emotion rose hot and thick in his throat, choking, ready to spill free.

No, no, no, no . . .

If they starved him and trapped him with a human, who knew how long he could fight his instinct to survive, how long before he became one of them . . . animals ruled by hunger?

Then he would be utterly and irrevocably lost. The fate his mother always feared would be his.

A flash of memory filled his head. A night long ago. A hundred years past. He lay in bed. A boy. His twin slept soundly beside him. The wind outside their mountain cottage howled, shaking the shutters. Only firelight illuminated the sparse confines.

His mother emerged over the two of them, a knife poised, ready to strike. Then she crumbled, sobbing, unable to kill the pair of demons she had spawned. He had watched her from thinly parted eyes as she staggered across the room and dropped to the hearth before the fire, the dagger still clutched in her hand. He knew then. Knew that whatever he was didn't deserve life.

Unfortunate that she had not found the strength

of will. Unfortunate that a mere knife would not have ended his life. For he now sat a prisoner in a rotting cell . . . waiting for the beast within to surface and devour whatever hapless female they chose to toss at him. Maybe his mother should have finished him then and spared him—spared the world.

Emotion burned through him, incinerating all shields he had constructed. He could no longer fight it. Closing his eyes, he rolled his head against the cold wall, unable to stop the despair from flowing free.

PALACIOS, TEXAS

Rafe Santiago woke with a scream thick in his throat. Instantly, his wife was beside him, wrapping her arms around his sweat-dampened chest in a fierce hold.

"Rafe, what is it?"

"Sebastian," he spit out between gasps. "He's in trouble."

His eyes locked with Kit's. The green pulled him in, a calming balm to the stark horror he had just felt. His brother's horror. They had always felt a connection, a bond that could stretch across the ocean which separated them.

Seb had felt Rafe's turmoil when he turned Kit

into one of them—a hybrid lycan, a *dovenatu,* a rare species created through the mating of a lycan with a female descendant of Etienne Marshan—the world's first lycan.

Kit's voice swept through him. "Then we'll find him."

Slowly, he nodded. Rafe had been unable to reach his brother for months now. Not unusual. Sebastian was like that. Aloof. Solitary. He had broken free from Rafe years ago. Still, Rafe had suspected something was wrong. Whenever he tried to tap into his brother's head, he only got gray static.

He suspected. And now he knew.

Rising from the bed, he faced the window, staring down into the yard and beyond at the gently swelling waters of the bay. The swing on the porch where he and Kit sat after dinner creaked in the breeze.

"Did you . . . sense where he is?"

He recalled the dream, saw the awful room, felt Seb's pain, his battered body as if it were his own.

Seb's tormentor had spoken in Turkish. "Turkey. The last time I heard from him he was hunting a pack in Vienna. Something took him east. I can track him." He splayed a hand against the cool glass, fingers curling, pressing as though he would shatter the delicate barrier. "We'll need help."

He felt her move behind him. Her small hand

came to rest on his shoulder. His brother would never have been taken easily. Only an army of lycans could bring him down. They would need their own to go after him.

"Darius," he said.

"Gideon," she added.

He nodded. The four of them would be a force for any army to face, mortal or otherwise.

2

Ruby Deveraux woke with a sharp gasp tight in her throat. Her dream vanished like fast-fading smoke. She willed it gone, willed the frightening images and sensations from her head. She was good at that. Good at tossing up barriers.

Pulling the comforter tighter, she burrowed into the hotel bed, groaning as she eyed her murky surroundings. Sleep rarely gave her any sense of peace. How could it? Her defenses fell then. Dropped like a row of dominoes. Especially in a place teeming with people. Their thoughts and emotions hunted her in sleep, penetrated the closed shutters of her hotel room, finding her, becoming her own.

Rolling to her side, she inhaled the pungent aroma

of Turkish roses outside her window. Her dream clung, not yet ready to let go. A brutal shadowland of dark images that twisted with pain. Flashing teeth, snapping, tearing . . . rancid-hot breath on her neck.

She hadn't dreamed of monsters since she was a child. Not since her father deserted her. The months following that had been fraught with nightmares.

Still tired, she chafed her palms against the side of her face. In a few days, she would be on a plane home. Soon she would be safe in her house again. Safe and blessedly alone.

Sighing, she dragged a hand through her loosened hair and rolled her head side-to-side on the pillow, stretching her neck. Nothing would lure her from her hotel room tonight. The peanut butter crackers in her luggage would work for dinner. She needed to gather her energy to face the onslaught of tomorrow. Airports were never fun. Plenty of negative energy there.

Adele had been right. An empath should never stray too far from home. But Ruby had insisted she could handle it. The constant throb at her temples told her how wrong she had been. She should never have agreed to the trip. It wasn't like back home, when she could leave and escape the solitude of her farmhouse. Adele had warned her, tried to tell her there would be nowhere to run, but Ruby hadn't listened.

This trip had been important. A grand gesture of rebellion—freedom. Something she had to do to give back, to help girls like her. Like the girl she once had been.

The sunset call to prayer rang outside her hotel, vibrating the window's shutters. Solemn and dark . . . almost like everything else in this foreign land.

The familiar urge to flee seized her. Maybe she could catch a late-night flight out of Istanbul. She could be back in Louisiana tomorrow.

The rattle of a key in the lock had her peering at the door. Rosemary entered. The retired social worker looked closer to seventy than her fifty years. Hard lines edged her eyes and mouth, and when Ruby stared at her she felt only her weariness, her deep dissatisfaction with the world. *Defeat. Sourness.* It pulled her down, weighed her into the hotel bed.

Moving about the room, kicking off her shoes, Rosemary studied her for a long moment. "Rough day?"

Only two people knew of Ruby's . . . *gift*. Rosemary, who placed her in home after home. And Adele Summers, her best friend. Her only friend in Beau Rivage. Everyone else just wrote her off as the weird eccentric who lived on the old Deveraux farm.

She nodded weakly. "Yeah."

"I thought bringing you along as a chaperone wouldn't work." She sighed and Ruby felt the full bitter wave of her disgust. It wasn't new. Rosemary often felt disgusted with her over the years, mostly due to Ruby's inability to keep a foster family. She grimaced. Families had never wanted her once they realized what she was.

"I can't hide away forever." God knew she had hidden long enough.

"Well, what good are you to yourself or the girls when you get exhausted before noon? You should have stayed holed up at your farm."

Ruby swallowed down the lump in her throat. True. What kind of chaperone was she if she had to hide away instead of chaperoning the girls?

"What are you doing here? I hope you didn't skip dinner to check on me."

"I wouldn't do that. I came back here to look for Amy and Emily. Hoped they were in their rooms."

Ruby frowned. "Shouldn't they be at dinner?"

"*Should* is the operative word. I just checked their room. They both complained of stomach aches and took a cab back here earlier." She shook her head. "Those two. I never thought I'd ever have a kid under my care that could give me more grief than you, but they take the prize."

Ruby sat up, ignoring the jibe. "You believed they

both had a stomach ache? And you let them return on their own?"

"I didn't want to miss the tour of the Blue Mosque." Rosemary's eyes glinted defensively. "And they did share a plate at lunch today." She shrugged. "Maybe it was food poisoning."

"Right." Ruby swung her legs over the edge of the bed and pushed to her feet. Amy was a good girl, but easily misguided. Ever since she paired up with Emily, Amy had turned into someone else. A perfect parrot of the wilder Emily.

She hastily put on her shoes. "We should have split those two up from day one."

"Should," Rosemary said again. "That word comes up a lot with these kids."

Ruby resisted reminding her that the word *should* needed to be applied to the parents who brought children into the world and then failed them. Rosemary always had a way of blaming the kids. "I suggested you split them up."

Ruby had been one of them. Rejected. Abandoned. Left to the system. Ruby knew. She knew well.

"Any idea where they went?"

"Kevin said they were talking to some older guys earlier when we were browsing tapestries at the Bazaar. They invited them to a party. He heard the girls agree to meet them at six at that *pastirma* shop where we ate."

A party in a strange, exciting city. A pair of fifteen-year-old girls. Older exotic men. Great. It was a formula for disaster. Rising, she faced Rosemary. "Ready?"

She blinked. "Where are we going?"

"To get them."

The social worker's face screwed tight and she waved a hand. "They'll be fine . . . probably drag in after they've had their fun."

"And you're okay with that? What if they don't? What if they get into trouble? Or hurt?"

"Look. I'm not about to scour the city for them. And I don't know why you think I would."

"Oh, I don't know. Because it's your job."

"I don't get paid enough for that."

"Fine," Ruby bit out. "Where's John? I'll get him to go with me."

"Don't bother. He can't leave the rest of the kids to go off after two troublemakers."

She inhaled deeply. "All right. I'll go alone. I'll find them and bring them back."

"How?" Rosemary glanced at her watch. "You'll never make it there by six. The traffic—"

"Maybe." If she could get close enough it would be enough. She just had to get close enough. Her *gift* would do the rest.

Rosemary shot her a skeptical glare, and Ruby read the doubt there. More than that. She felt it. As always. Buried beneath Rosemary's general ennui and dissatisfaction with her life was her skepticism that Ruby could do nothing more than hide away in her farmhouse—the oddball loner everyone thought her. "You don't do crowds."

"I'll be back soon." She clicked her money belt into place around her waist, beneath her tank. Adele had bought it for her, insisting she wear it instead of using a handbag, so that her money, passport and visa never left her body.

"The girls will be long gone by the time you get there," Rosemary predicted. The bed creaked as she lowered her square, solid frame onto it.

Maybe. But not what they left behind. Not the lingering trace of their emotions. Not their blind, youthful enthusiasm. She should be able to feel them, track them. As long as she lowered her guard and let them in . . .

Rosemary continued. "You're wasting your time. They'll be back sometime tonight."

Ruby placed one hand to the door's latch. "I can't do that." Without another thought, she stepped out into the hall, into the waiting world with all its people, all its pain, ready to sink their teeth into her.

3

"Wait here, I'll be right back," Ruby instructed the cab driver before hurrying out into the labyrinth of streets, into a fog of spices and herbs.

In the fading dusk, she scanned the narrow streets for Amy's blond hair, bypassing the *pastirma* café where they ate earlier. Seeing nothing, she closed her eyes and released a deep breath . . . and let it all flow in. Every vile, poisoned sensation. Good existed, too. *Amusement. Joy.* But those faded amid the onslaught of negative feelings. The mean, the ugly, the sinister—they always hit harder.

She staggered from the force of emotions swirling around in the sultry air, bombarding her in wave after wave, eddying along her senses. Her stomach twisted and knotted. There was little time to process. Closing her eyes, she breathed thinly through her nose, swimming through the thick fog, searching until she located the girls.

She found them.

Emily and Amy. *Excitement. Eagerness. Pride.*

It thrilled them to have attracted the notice of *men*. They knew they were being bad, breaking the rules. But they reveled in it too much to stop themselves.

Ruby walked, following the heady sense of euphoria the girls emitted. Ferry horns blew low and deep from the nearby port. Eyes thinly parted, she pushed ahead, following only her awareness of them. She strode from the center of the bazaar quarter, down a street of busy shoppers vying with vendors for their evening fare.

Mingled with Emily and Amy's emotions lurked those of their companions. Two of them. Ruby's stomach knotted and clenched. She had never felt anything like them before. The sensation they emitted was more of a condition than a feeling. *Black hunger. A mawing ache.* And in that hunger, nothing else existed. *Bleak emptiness.* And that was even more frightening. Because there should be something. Some feeling. Some sentiment. There always was. She could always feel something. No one felt nothing. It simply wasn't human to feel nothing, to possess only that unnatural hunger. Even a starved man must have other thoughts in his head, feelings in his heart. But these men with Amy . . . they felt empty. Dead.

Weaving through the warren of streets, Ruby's stomach twisted tighter. She had to reach the girls. Fast.

She shook her head as one determined vendor waggled a dead chicken in her face. Pushing ahead. Ruby tuned everything else out as she clung to the thread of emotions from the girls. Dodging a cyclist, she hurried. The thread suddenly grew thinner. Gasping, she jerked to a stop. Looking left and right, she concentrated. Listening to her instinct, she ducked into a small side street.

Sheer curtains billowed off windows high overhead as she hurried down the narrow cobbled street. The market's volume faded to a dull purr behind her, and the thread grew stronger again.

She passed an old lady. Sitting on the stoop of her building, she stared out at Ruby with night-black eyes and spat something in Arabic from lips that moved as quickly as the fingers shelling chickpeas into a bowl.

A sense of urgency stole over her and Ruby quickened her pace. Tenements reached for the sky on either side of her. A baby cried from inside the one to her left, the wail stretching and twisting into the twilight until it died suddenly.

She stopped abruptly amid the growing shadows as the street came to an end at a courtyard. A fountain sat at its center, its gurgling water the only sound in the silence of impending night. A warehouse-type building sat within the courtyard, a squat, solid structure that crouched wide in the shadow of tenements. With its massive double doors of ancient wood, it looked nearly as old as the city itself.

The skin of her face tingled, stomach queasy with knowing. Amy and Emily were behind those doors.

The same black wave of hunger she had felt earlier swamped her as she faced the building. *Aching. Craving.* Only stronger. Only more. Fighting back the nausea welling up inside her, she approached the door and rapped until her knuckles burned. Her knocking ricocheted off the courtyard around her.

Moments passed before the door opened. A man stood there, his dusky-skinned face curiously ageless. "Yes?" he asked, blue-green eyes glittering against his camel-toned skin.

She moistened dry lips. "Hi. Two of my friends are guests here. We were invited to a party—"

Suspicion. Anxiety. He pasted a smile of welcome on his face, despite his tension. "Ah, yes. Of course." He stepped aside, waving her in.

She stepped inside a mosaic-tiled foyer, not at all what she expected given the building's dismal exterior. Congratulating herself on the ease in which she had infiltrated, she looked expectantly at the man, wondering at his unease over her arrival.

"The young ladies are this way."

She followed him, trying not to stare at the opulence around her. Surely nothing the girls—or herself—had seen in their corner of Louisiana. The paintings on the wall, the gilded chandelier, the ageless sculpture set upon a strategically placed marble pedestal.

The soles of her sneakers fell flat on the tiled floor. She clung to the jumpy thread of emotions that ran a direct line to Amy and Emily. Harmless compared to the dark ache swirling on the air. *Desperate need.* Thick as smoke, suffocating, threatening to drag her down and make her sick. As sick and helpless as she used to get when she was a kid, before she learned control, before she learned to set up her barriers. She sucked in a deep breath.

They stopped before a door of carved pewter inset with opals. The beauty of it almost distracted from the fact that it was bolted on the outside. The man sent her a smile, knocking once before lifting the hefty bolt with a grunt. The smile might have disarmed her if she did not sense unease tripping through him . . . and a skittery sense of urgency. He wanted to run away, to flee . . .

Why? What would he have to be afraid of?

Then the door opened.

Clawing hunger. A pulling ache.

Struggling past the strange . . . condition—*not a feeling; there was no feeling, no sentiment*—she spotted Amy laughing on a couch, sipping champagne and talking to a pair of very attentive men.

And Ruby couldn't go anywhere. Couldn't leave.

She cleared the threshold, noting with some relief that the room was crowded with men and women alike. It was a party. That much was true, at least. Softer, milder emotions existed beneath the hunger. *Glee. Delight. Levity.* All too light to make much of an impression on her. The black ache eclipsed everything else.

Music filled the room. Blood-pumping hip-hop piped in from an overhead system. A huge spread of food and drink weighed down one table, which everyone appeared to be sampling, making the hunger even more puzzling.

Ruby drove a hard line toward Amy.

"Ruby," she cried. *Annoyance. Guilt.* "What are you doing here?" Amy looked over her shoulder, as if she expected to see Rosemary and John in tow.

"I've come to take you and Emily back to the hotel."

Emily arrived then, one hand propped on her hip. "We're not going," she announced. *Hostility. Aggression.*

"Oh, yes you are," Ruby countered. "You are fif-teen years—"

"Ruby, is it?" A man stepped in front of her. Tall, dark, his eyes glittered an eerie silver. Hunger swathed him. Controlled. Careful. And beneath that . . . the familiar nothing. *Emptiness.* An animal that did not feel emotion, only the physical demands of his body. *Hunger.* She resisted the impulse to retreat a step.

"I'm Gunter. Why not stay and chaperone the girls? Eat. Drink. Be our guest."

It was like coming face-to-face with a serpent. Charm and hospitality dripped from his voice, but be-hind it all—a void. His expression exuded warmth . . . but Ruby knew. She *felt.* Something dreadfully, terribly wrong flowed from him. From nearly everyone else in this room. She darted a quick glance around. Several others gazed at her. Her breath caught at their silver eyes. How the hell was it possible for them to *all* have the same freakish eyes?

"Amy," she whispered, her lips barely moving as her hand inched toward the girl. Her pulse raced at her neck. "Come with me. Now."

"Why don't *you* beat it?" Emily snapped beside a very big leather-clad tattooed man who looked old enough to be her father. "Amy doesn't need you for a mother. Why don't you go have a kid of your own and stop trying to mother us?"

Ruby's gaze crept back to the man, the serpent. Gunter cocked his head, studying her as though she were some rare specimen, a field mouse to devour. But something in his look struck her as familiar. It was a look she had seen before—regardless that it came from a pair of unnatural eyes.

It was the look she received when someone realized she was not what she seemed, not quite right, not normal. He knew it. He saw that. Her father gave her that look. Her grandparents. Her kindergarten teacher. On occasion, even her mother had looked at her that way.

"It's too late to go now. You will stay," he purred in his thick accent, staring down at her with glinting eyes. "I shall enjoy you, I think."

The door closed shut then. The sound of the bolt falling into place on the other side sent a vibration straight to her heart. The servant was gone.

Amy's breath changed beside her, released in a nervous titter. A shaky smile curved her mouth.

"Open those doors," Ruby demanded.

"I can't." Gunter lifted one shoulder in a mild shrug. "It's locked from the outside."

"Chill out, Ruby." Despite the flip words, Ruby felt the niggle of unease worming through Amy. She needed to build on that, needed to get the girl on board with her so they could get out of this. Whatever *this* was . . .

"Freak out enough?" Emily rolled her eyes and turned back to her tattooed friend.

"Sit. Relax. Enjoy." Gunter waved to the table behind them, very much the host. "Have something to eat. The fun is about to begin."

Ruby pressed close to Amy. "What kind of fun?"

"Oh . . . entertainment. If you would excuse me a moment." With an enigmatic smile, he left them to talk to someone else.

Ruby wrapped a hand around Amy's arm, vowing to never let go. Whatever happened. And something was about to happen. A thread of expectation laced the air. *Readiness*. Faint but there.

Emily lounged on a couch on the other side of the room now, smoking a cigarette with a growing collection of admirers.

Ruby swept her gaze over the room. No windows. Just enclosed space and stale air that swirled with tobacco smoke and a heavy shot of black hunger. That hunger deepened. Swallowing the strange void of before.

"Amy, we have to get out of here." The girl's skin quivered beneath her grasp. *Apprehension. Fear.* "Something really bad is going to happen."

Loneliness. Regret. "I think you're right," Amy whispered.

"You're not alone, Amy," she assured, flexing her

fingers around the girl's slim arm, as though she could inject comfort with the promise. "I'm here. I'm with you."

Surprise. Amy's wide eyes locked with Ruby. *Relief.* Biting her bottom lip, she nodding. "Yeah." Her nodding increased as if she grew strength from Ruby's pledge. "Yeah. Okay. How? How are we going to get out of here?"

Scanning the room, that question echoed with a chill down her spine. Her gaze snagged on a vent set high in the wall. She shook her head. Everyone would notice the two of them clawing the wall to climb through the air duct. Still, it was a way out . . .

The air in the room changed subtly, shifted. The laughter ceased. Voices turned, lifted, took on an edge. *Confusion. Alarm.*

She dropped her gaze from the vent, feeling the rising hysteria, marking it in the faces of those that backed away from some of the others, people that seemed to be . . . sick. Whatever was happening to them, they reveled in it. *Exhilaration. Pleasure-pain, sharp as a blade.* They writhed, hunkered at the waists, faces contorting as though in great torment. Glass shattered. Someone pounded at the door.

Amy stepped toward one man, her hand outstretched to lend help. "Are you—"

Brutal, clawing need spilled from the stranger.

"Amy, no!" Ruby tugged the girl back.

Amy pulled free and bent over the man, laying one small hand over his back. "He needs help!"

Fear. Ruby tasted it. Bitter and acrid in her mouth.

Desperate, she latched onto the teenager's hand again. "The only one right now who needs help is us!" Even not understanding what was happening, she understood enough to run. In the cramping, twisting pit of her belly, she knew they were in danger.

Her gaze swept the walls again, over the bolted door, searching frantically, as though a window would appear that had not been there before.

She ran her tongue over the edge of her teeth, the fear a coppery tang there.

Then pain slammed into her, bowing her over with a scream.

Something warm tickled the top of her lip. Her fingers flew there, brushing wetness. Pulling her hand back, blood covered her fingertips. Her stomach cramped harder. She only suffered nosebleeds around another's pain. Acute physical pain.

Her gaze again landed on the screened air duct at the same moment screams ripped over the thrum of voices. More pain rose up then, acrid as burnt feathers, and she moved.

"Amy! Amy! C'mon!" She shoved the table laden with drink and food against the wall, but it was too late. A glance over her shoulder revealed Amy—what remained of her—engulfed in a man's arms. Covered in blood.

Only he was no longer a man at all.

None of them were.

4

Where men once stood, grotesque creatures crashed throughout the room, snarling, hissing, destroying furniture . . . destroying life.

Large and beast-like. Brown, black, tawny-red. Their faces twisted with engorged bones, fierce and hideous. Monstrosities.

Clawed fists ripped into guests who laughed and drank only moments ago.

Pain. Pain. Pain.

Their agony drowned her. Her knees buckled and she grabbed the edge of the table to stop from falling. Blood coursed from her nose, running over her lips, dripping down her chin.

Swiping at her mouth so she didn't swallow, she

pressed herself into the hard edge of the table and clung, shaking from the pain, from the brutal sledge-hammer of death after death.

Dark spots danced before her eyes. Blackness threatened, trying to pull her in—an escape from the overwhelming agony.

One of the beasts caught her in his sights. She felt his awareness of her, his excitement, his rush of conquest. *Gunter*. He no longer looked like a man, but she knew.

Her mouth dried, a scream trapped in her lungs as the monster charged her, launching over his fellow brethren busy mauling the victims caught in their clutches. That black hunger reached her, stronger, darker, crazed in its absolute power.

Another guest, arms flailing with panic as she tried to escape, staggered between Ruby and the on-coming creature. Ruby ducked and slid beneath the table, cringing as the woman's scream added to the screeching din of misery . . . a scream that could have been hers. Might as well have been her own for the pain that twisted inside her. White-hot torment sur-rounded her and urged her to curl into as tight a ball as possible and vanish. Disappear.

Only she couldn't.

Sucking in a deep breath, she crawled atop the table, her movements rushed, clumsy. Standing, her hands brushed the screen. So close. On her tiptoes, she wedged her fingers beneath the screen and wall and yanked the thin metal sheet free, sending the tiny screws flying.

Adrenaline fed her with a strength she did not know she possessed as she pulled herself up. Arms quivering, she hefted herself inside the narrow air duct.

Air sawed from her lips in deep pain-filled drags as she crawled. She didn't dare stop to rest. To think. To regain her breath. Her elbows slammed against metal as she worked.

Heart hammering, pulse racing, she swiped again at her bleeding nose. Pain still chased her. If she didn't escape, she'd probably bleed to death. If the monsters didn't get to her first.

Hot tears streamed her face as she crawled. Every fiber of her being ached, screaming as she moved at feverish speed.

She dragged herself along, not knowing where she headed, only caring that she moved away from the slaughter, the pain and fiendish creatures that she could not yet wrap her thoughts around.

It seemed like hours. Cold air washed over her flesh. The narrow tunnel shook, vibrating with the cries and screams of those left behind. Pain trailed her, dug deep into her bones.

She reached another vent. Peering though the screen, she eyed below, recognizing the area from earlier—mosaic tiles, the great front room she had passed through after entering the building. *Empty.* Palms out, she shoved the screen free. It clattered to the ground below, and she waited, holding her ragged breath in the silence, half expecting, half fearing those same creatures would charge into the room like hounds alerted.

Hearing nothing, she slowly stuck out her head. The duct was too small for her to turn her body around, so she had to grit her teeth and plunge out into the room, praying she did not break her neck.

She fell shoulder first onto the cushioned seat of an armchair, breaking it into several pieces. Amid the broken furniture, she clambered to her feet and rushed to the front door, ready to burst free into the night, away from the madness, the nightmare from which she would wake at any moment.

She felt him before he grabbed her.

Elation. Thrill.

A hard hand spun her around and she faced the same man who had led her into that cesspit of carnage and then bolted the door. "How did you escape?"

He began pulling her deeper into the building. She resisted, envisioning him tossing her back in that room. Despite his slim frame, he was stronger. Her heels slid over the slick floor.

"This is a first. No one has escaped before. Very clever of you. They're going to be furious, though." He scowled. "Now what am I going to do with you?"

"No!" she screamed as she fought, crazed. He would have to kill her before forcing her back in with those . . . things. With so much torture and agony. And death.

She could almost hear Adele's voice. *This is why you should have stayed put in Beau Rivage. You have no business moving about in the world.*

Just as her grandmother claimed all those years ago following her mother's funeral service, only not as harsh as her: *You should be locked up.*

In a final surge of strength, she stomped on his foot and bolted.

She didn't get far. He tackled her from behind, the force sending her tumbling with a hard smack onto the floor. Flipping her over, he glared down at her.

"I won't go back in that room." She would not experience those deaths again. Not the pain. Not if she could help it. "I won't go back in there. I won't!" Her voice rang shrill.

Tsking his tongue, he explained, "I can't open those doors until sunrise. I wouldn't be fool enough to risk my own life."

It all happened slowly then. She watched his fingers curl into a fist.

"But I can't let you go. For now, this should be sufficient. They will be pleased with me in this at least."

Pain exploded in her face, then . . . nothing.

"I can't imagine how she escaped, Master. No one has ever done so before."

Ruby did not stir even as the voice with the plaintive edge penetrated the heavy fog in her head. She froze every muscle, held her breath and waited, thinking, trying to assess her situation with her eyes closed. Her face ached, especially the area below her right eye.

"That doesn't mean no one could. Some ingenious soul committed enough to survival would eventually have done so." Footsteps drew closer. "She knew something was amiss the moment she arrived in the room. You should never have let her pass through the door, Conrad. We've survived all these years by avoiding surprises . . . and sticking to protocol."

A soft mattress cushioned her. Apparently the loyal retainer had been kind enough to place her on a bed after he knocked her out.

She listened, opening herself up to the emotions swirling around her, gauging the danger. Beneath the servant's ingratiating need to please, a wire-tight unease hummed from him, as if he knew he dealt with a wild animal that at any moment might turn deadly.

His master spoke again, voice sharp with reprimand. "You should never have brought her in after the door was bolted."

"But, Master, she came looking for two of the girls. I thought it best to let her in. What if—"

"I don't keep you on to think, Conrad." *Annoyance.* "Follow my bidding and do not act of your own accord again. Do you understand?"

"Yes, Master." A sigh followed the subdued comment. *Resignation. Relief.* "I checked her identification. She's American."

She stifled the urge to reach for her money belt and check if it still remained on her body. The impulse quickly fled at the sudden hand on her leg.

Avarice. Lust. "Let me have her. She smells fresh. I bet she's a virgin."

A female snorted and Ruby felt her disdain as sharp as a knife to her neck. "A virgin? What's wrong with her?"

The truth hit a nerve. Her curse prevented her from becoming close with any man. *Intimate.* She had tried. Her record was four dates. Then she either ran, spooked by emotions she picked up over dessert: boredom, or worse—lust. The guys who spent the entire date in a state of arousal sent her running for the hills. The bored ones, the safe ones, she stuck with, hoping she could evoke their interest. Eventually. She inevitably ran them off, her *gift* manifesting and scaring them away.

Like the time she stopped her date from biting into his burger. He'd been rude to the waiter, and from the hovering server's anxious glee, she had sensed he'd done something to the burger. When she had knocked the burger from Derek's hand, he looked at her as though she were a freak and never called again.

"Can she not attract a man?" the female sneered.

"She has no failings there." The touch on her leg lifted, moving to her breast, sending her flying up on the bed. Nothing could make her to suffer that.

She scrambled close to the headboard, eyeing the room's four occupants.

The bastard—Conrad—who had cold-cocked her blinked in surprise. The other three, two men and a woman, seemed more intrigued than surprised. Heads angled, they observed her as if she were some sort of carnival exhibit, their gazes an eerie silver that glowed in the sunlit room. They filled her with coldness, as if ice hardened their veins. She recognized Gunter instantly.

"You," she breathed, throat tightening as the memory of him shifting into a beast froze her heart cold.

He nodded, a scary smile fixed to his face. "Sleep well? Sorry you had to rush out last night. You missed a lovely party."

A curse rose on her tongue, ready to fly, but it never fell. Tears burned her eyes as the memory of last night—Amy—slammed into her, locking her in fresh horror.

Her gaze slid over each of them. She spied an open door just beyond Conrad's left. She vaulted toward it.

Hard arms locked around her waist. Her legs flailed, kicking wildly in the air. Her captor laughed. The hollow sound scraped her nerves, echoing the humming silence she felt from him. *Nothingness. Bleak desolation.*

"Put her down, Yusuf." The silver-eyed devil released her, his hands sliding off her body with agonizing slowness.

She dropped on the edge of the bed.

Yusuf smoothed back his long hair and repeated the familiar request. "Give her to me. I like her fight."

"Enough with your selfish desires." Gunter sliced a hand through the air. "You should be well sated after last night. I have another plan for her."

The ominous words shivered down her spine. Ruby dug her fingers into the mattress, a fingernail cracking from the pressure, not liking the sudden intent look coming over Gunter's face.

"W-what?" she managed to get out, feeling every bit of his satisfaction. His self-congratulatory attitude swept through her, raising the tiny hairs at her neck.

"Have no fear," he assured her in mocking tones, moving toward her, one hand outstretched. She cringed at the sight of his long nails, buffed to a pink sheen. "You may have missed last night's fun. But I have something even better planned for you. I've been looking for a special female, and I'm convinced you're just the one."

5

Sebastian raised his head at the sound of the door unlocking. Gunter entered the cell's dank confines, impeccably dressed, hair neat and crisp from a recent shower. And yet he brought with him the odor of death. Last night's kills clung to him, imbedded in his pores as he moved into the room.

With the glow of dusk fading from the small window set high in the wall, Sebastian knew the second night of moonrise neared. He marked it in the pull of his bones, in their overwhelming urge to bend and stretch. Especially with the aroma of freshly spilled blood sinking down to his cell. Wicked and enticing to the hunger clenching his stomach. He had heard the cries last night. Smelled the blood of the fallen. It had only intensified his misery.

And it was misery. Like nothing he'd known before. The beast had never felt so alive, so ready to break free. He never turned unless he willed it. Unless he wanted it to happen.

Annika sank down beside him and lowered those beautiful, cruel hands to his bare flesh. "I've missed you, pet."

"I bet," he bit out.

Then he noticed the girl. Smelled her.

One of Gunter's soldiers dragged her forward by a single wrist. The human struggled, dark hair tossing wildly as she kicked, feet scrabbling, grappling for ground.

Gunter snapped his fingers.

The henchman flung her into the center of the room. She fell hard, a crumpled ragdoll in a heap.

His body jerked to life. He stopped himself from surging against the chains, sagging back against the wall, appearing unmoved, unaffected. His gaze narrowed on the woman. Her head was bowed, dark hair a mess obscuring her face. Her back lifted, shoulders rising and falling with ragged breaths. Her khaki slacks and red tank top screamed tourist. Easy bait for these fiends.

"A gift for you," Gregory announced.

Sebastian understood at once.

He forced ice into his veins, blankness into his stare. Gunter had made his intentions clear days ago. Sebastian, starving away in this cell, had not forgotten. He had wondered when his victim would arrive, and if he would be too far gone to stop from killing her.

"Never say I didn't give you anything. Yusuf here wanted her for himself."

He shifted, his chains clanking. "Then let him keep her. Just get her the fuck out of here," Sebastian growled, rising up, crouching on the bare pads of his feet, iron manacles cutting into the raw, exposed flesh of his wrists. But he didn't feel the pain. Not anymore. Only hunger. A deep, gnawing hunger. His mouth watered, nostrils quivering, catching her sweet scent.

"She's a waste on this mongrel," Yusuf spat out.

"Silence," Gunter declared in a biting voice, glittering eyes communicating the reminder that he was the alpha of the pack. What Yusuf thought failed to signify.

Turning back to Sebastian, he smiled again. "I could have tossed you some wretched piece of mankind." He stepped further into the room, one hand reaching down to stroke the liquid-dark hair of the woman who had yet to lift her head and reveal her face. Was she demented? Or had they broken her already so that she couldn't think? Didn't care? "Instead, I give you this. Tempting, isn't she? Appetizing." Laughter laced his voice. "However will you resist?" He addressed Annika, nodding once. "Now."

Annika unlocked his manacles. They fell from the blood-slicked bones of his wrists and ankles. Only he didn't feel the relief he should. He snatched at the irons, as if he could put them back on. Annika hastily stepped clear of him.

"No!" he shouted, surging to his feet. He couldn't be free to move in this cell with a human. Not in his condition.

Gunter laughed. He lifted his hand. The girl's dark hair fell like water through his fingers. "Enjoy." He moved to the door, Yusuf and Annika preceding him. His chuckle grated on Sebastian's tightly strung nerves.

"Take her with you," Sebastian shouted.

Gunter's gaze clung to his for a moment before the door banged shut, leaving Sebastian alone with the female.

Free of his chains, he staggered to the door, pounding it with his fists until they felt like two boneless hunks of flesh.

His stomach tightened and twisted, its clawing pain refusing to let him forget his hunger. He had not eaten in days. His strength was low . . . along with his will. And now he had this to contend with. *Her.* Weeks had passed since Gunter announced his intention to starve him and force him into feeding. How much longer could he last?

Turning, he did not move from the door. With his back pressed to the hard length, he watched as she rose to her knees, his gut tightening with her every motion. She lifted her head, staring at him from tangled strands of hair. She shoved the hair from her face and sent it rippling down her back. She watched him carefully, her pretty face guarded, bright splotches burning her cheeks at the sight of his nudity.

"You're not one of them," she declared, looking away.

He drilled her with his gaze, finding her eyes through the murk . . . a deep brown, not quite as dark as her hair. Flecks of gold surrounded her irises. Shards of amber buried in dark earth. It'd be a shame to watch the life fade there. An even greater shame to be the one responsible for that loss of life.

He registered her fear, felt it on the stagnant air, tasted it with a salivating mouth. Not so different from a wolf in the wild. Sniffing out their prey.

Blood smeared her face, a dark brown stain beneath her nose, nudging her pretty lips. She pushed to her feet, wincing. Her hand brushed a bruised cheek as though movement gave her pain.

"Stay where you are," he growled, his voice thick and garbled, warning him just how close he was to losing control. She smelled so sweet. Creamy vanilla. And looked even better. A feast for his eyes.

Her mouth was almost too full, plump and moist, bringing on a surge of carnal images. Those luscious pink lips surrounding him, drawing him in deep. The image sent a bolt of need straight to his cock, waking that part of him that had betrayed him so many times over the last months. After the savage treatment Gunter's bitches had dealt him, he wondered how he could even hunger for a woman again.

A cruel smile twisted his lips. The first tasty bit of mortal to cross his path and his blood pumped hard. Just spoke to the resilience of his species. No one was forcing him to crave her now. Not the impending moonrise. Not even the hunger clawing his insides. It was simply his body's natural response.

She sucked in a sharp breath. The color in her cheeks deepened . . . almost as though she read his mind. Impossible. She was not him, or a lycan, capable of sensing things outside a human's natural range of ability. More than likely it had to do with his raging erection.

He inhaled her from across the room. If her clothes hadn't already told him, her scent did. She was foreign to these parts. Hadn't even been here long enough to soak up any of the odors. She came from somewhere else. She smelled of ripe woman and earth and something else, something he had never come across before in all his years . . . clean and woodsy, warm wind-blown hills, whisky-sweet.

He felt her stare land on his wrists and ankles. Even in the deepening dusk, she couldn't make out the full extent of the damage . . . couldn't see the exposed bone and shredded flesh. "Are you all right?"

When she made a move toward him, his pulse spiked against his throat and he knew he was not all right. And she wasn't either. Not if she kept coming toward him.

"Stop right there," he barked.

She froze. Her gaze traveled his shoulders and torso, skimming over the dried blood stark against his skin. "You're hurt." She made a move toward him again.

He threw a hand up in the air. "No." The word fell like a loud clap of thunder.

She stilled, shaking her head.

He closed his hand into a tight fist. "Keep away from me. Don't come near." His nails dug into his palms until he felt his blood flow against his fingers.

Long moments passed before she spoke again. "But you're hurt. I can feel—" she stopped abruptly. "I can tell. I can tell that you're injured. Did one of them attack you?" She strode forward and splayed a hand over his chest, where one of the bitches had scratched and bit him days ago. He'd already healed, only blood remained.

His breath escaped in a hiss at the delicious sting of her warm palm over him. "Don't touch me."

She felt good. Warm. Alive. Female. Not like the females who ravaged him body and soul these many weeks, but soft, tender. Woman. Mortal. Closing his eyes, he inhaled the clean scent of her hair, vanilla-scented shampoo . . . it echoed on her skin and his mouth watered.

He closed a hand around her wrist, squeezing. "I'm not hurt."

She placed her other hand on his chest, probing gently, trailing it over him as though searching for injuries. "But there's blood. Everywhere."

"It's old," he gritted. "It's dried."

She shook her head.

"Look," he growled, turning so that he slammed her against the wall. He shoved his face close to hers. "You haven't a clue what you've gotten yourself into here."

Her wide gaze scanned him, staring intently at him beneath ink dark brows. Anger glowed in her eyes. "I've got a pretty good idea. I lost my friends. I watched them get eaten by a bunch of monsters—"

"Lycans."

"What?"

"Lycans," he said, with more patience than he felt. "Werewolves."

"Werewolves," she echoed, glancing to the high-set window. Faint moonglow spilled inside their prison.

"That's right. Last night was a full moon. And tonight."

Her gaze returned to him then, as piercing as before. Looking so deeply, so probing, intent in a way no mortal had ever looked upon him before. A flicker of unease tripped through him. Something was different about her . . .

"Will they come for us tonight?"

He shook his head. "They have other plans for us."

Between the press of their bodies, her hand brushed his chest, directly over his heart. "You're not one of them. How did you escape them? How come we're down here?"

All good questions, but he was certain she wasn't ready for the answers.

Her words gained speed, rushing forward in her fear. "Are they saving us for later or something?"

In the distance, it began. Screams flowed down, breathing through the bones of the building, looking for escape. Buried beneath the warehouse, the tortured sounds echoed only faintly in his ears. To a mortal's ear—her ears—they would be undetectable.

"No," he spat, imagining the humans being ripped apart, devoured upstairs. "They're not saving us for later. They're seeing to their needs tonight."

A wild look swept over her. Unnatural. Her brown eyes gleamed, the dark centers dilating with an emotion he could not name. She shrugged out between him and the wall. Trembling, she edged away, reminding him of some woodland creature, eyes darting, her head cocked to the side as though she sensed . . . something.

He frowned. "What? What is it?" She couldn't possibly hear the distant screams.

Chafing her arms, her shaking worsened. Jamming her eyes shut, she ground out, "N-nothing."

He smelled it first. Then saw. Rich, wine-red blood escaped her nose in a seductive trickle.

His throat tightened, a wave of hunger washing over him. "You're bleeding."

She wiped at the sweet-smelling blood with the back of her hand. "It's nothing."

He licked dry lips. "Are you hurt?"

"No," she snapped, pressing her fingers to her nose. "Sometimes my nose bleeds. It'll stop soon." Opening her eyes, she looked up. Again, as if she knew more than she possibly could. As if she heard the sounds of death. Killing. Inhaling a steady breath, she fixed molten brown eyes on him. "How long have you been down here?" Her gaze scanned the scruffy growth of beard on his face.

"Long enough." He drew away along the wall, eyes devouring her, the fruit of temptation that he must resist. He *would* resist.

Her eyes followed him.

"Why do you . . . fear me?" she whispered.

Her words—the truth—sliced through him. There was no denying he feared her. He feared her before he ever knew her, when Gunter told him she would be coming. He feared what she would do to him. Drive him over the brink, steal his soul . . .

But how did she know that?

Then he understood.

Incredible as it seemed, she could read his mind. Somehow. Some way. Maybe she was a witch. He knew they existed, one had started the lycan curse.

"I'm not afraid of you," he lied.

He tried to clear his mind, to not think about the fear she roused. To not think about himself. About the beast that prowled inside him whose instinct refused to let him starve.

"Whatever." Sighing, she chafed her hands harder along her arms, clearly attempting to warm herself against the room's chill. She turned in a small circle, stopping to consider the window set high in the wall. Again. The window was narrow, not large enough for anybody to squeeze through.

"You won't fit."

She looked at him again. "I see that. What are we going to do, then?"

He dragged a ragged breath into his constricted lungs, battling her presence, battling the inner demon she awakened. "Do?"

"Yes, what's the plan?" She took a step in his direction, bringing her sweet scent closer.

"The plan," he gritted, sidling further away. A humorless smile twisted his mouth. Strange for him to fear *her* so much. He was stronger. More powerful. Experienced in ways this mortal—or witch—never could be. And still, she struck fear in the shadows of his heart. He would not become all that his mother feared and reviled.

"The plan is for you to keep your mouth shut. For you to stay on that side of the room and keep the hell away from me. Become invisible," he demanded. "And just maybe you'll live."

And maybe he wouldn't become the very thing he loathed and hunted.

6

Ruby watched the dark shape of the man over the tops of her bent knees. She flexed her fingers around her calves, locking her arms tighter, as if they were the only thing holding her together, keeping her from splintering apart.

Dark anguish rolled across the room like billowing smoke, stoking the core of her with a feeling she could not quite absorb . . . could not understand. Her stomach ached as it did whenever bombarded by too much emotion. Only it usually took a large group or crowd of people to affect her. Over the years, she had learned to block out individuals and small groups. But the feelings he emitted were too . . . much. Too intense. Too overwhelming.

She dropped her head against the cold stone wall at her back. Stay away from him? Right. Fat lot of good that did. She *felt* him. Every strange, twisted emotion roiling inside him. Feelings that reminded her of the beasts upstairs—lycans, he claimed. And yet not. Different. Less frightening but—crazy as it sounded—equally dangerous.

The strongest emotion he emitted was fear. Acerbic and nonstop, the bitter tang of it coated her mouth. Instead of making him weak, it only made him more dangerous. Unpredictable.

Before she could reconsider, she whispered into the still of the room, "Why can't we talk?" Because she needed to talk, needed to connect with someone amid this nightmare.

His bowed head snapped up. His eyes glittered at her from across the shadowed distance. Even in the darkness, she was careful to train her gaze on his bearded face. A handsome face, she thought. It was hard to tell. She knew he was naked, but in the darkness she could at least pretend not to know.

"What do you want to talk about? What can you possibly say that I want to hear? Want to share your sad story with me? Well, forget it. Everyone's got a sad story, and I don't need to hear yours."

She bit the inside of her cheek at his scathing tone and glanced away. His accent was faint, the intonation indecipherable but nothing she had heard in these parts. He wasn't Turkish, though. She felt sure of that. The harsh rasp of his breath filled the stretch of silence.

Inhaling, she faced him again. "You've clearly been down here awhile." She swallowed. "Like it or not, we're all we have right now."

He laughed, the sound terrible . . . the humor within him foul and awful. "I *don't* like it. Before, I just had *my* neck to look out for. Now I have yours, too."

Indignation swept through. "By all means, let me relieve you of your obligation to look out for me."

His lips curled back from his teeth to reveal a flash of straight white teeth. "I'm just that kind of guy. Call me old-fashioned."

She snorted. "I'm used to looking out for myself. I have no expectations that you're going to rescue me."

"As you said, we're stuck here. Together." A deep sigh rattled loose from him. "Hell." His arm lifted and she squinted into the gloom as he dragged a hand through his short-cropped hair, scratching fiercely at his head. "Very well. Why don't you tell me about yourself?"

Wariness rippled through her. Even as he asked the question, she sensed he didn't want to know anything about her. He didn't want to know her. Caginess and dislike seeped from him. "Suddenly you're interested?"

He sighed again, and she felt a new emotion rise. Something resembling desperation. "To pass the time, sure. Go ahead. Talk. Tell me how you came to be here." He hesitated. "Tell me who you are." His desperation reached across to her, a toxic fume. Urgent and grim. So much that she felt inclined to appease him.

"My name is Ruby Deveraux."

"You're American. What are you doing in Turkey?"

She rubbed her aching temples. "It's complicated."

"We've got time."

"I volunteered to act as a chaperone for a group of foster kids. They got a grant for this trip but needed chaperones that could pay their own way . . ." her voice faded. Those details weren't important.

"You've got to be kidding," he muttered. "You're some sort of damn Mary Poppins?"

"I'm not—"

"Right."

"Hardly. I just . . ." she paused for breath. "I was a foster kid. After my mother died. This is something I wanted to do. It's not my job or anything."

"Oh, not a job. You're a true altruist, then. Yeah. Not Poppins at all." He made a low, animal-like sound in his throat. "So what do you do when you're not escorting lost little souls through Europe?"

"I own a catering business." Work she loved, a vocation she could do in the safety of her home, private, alone, hidden from the world except during the brief time she emerged to deliver her food. And cooking made her feel better, connected to the mother who loved her as no one else had. The best moments of her life were of them in the kitchen. Baking cookies, fresh fruit cobblers. Crawdaddies in the sink. A big pot of gumbo on the stove.

"What kind of food?"

"Down-home. Southern. Barbecue. Some fusion. I'm not classically trained, but cooking is something I picked up from my mother and kept at after she died. After high school, culinary school just made sense."

"And how old were you when your mother died?"

"Fourteen."

"And you were in foster care after that?"

The skin of her face tightened at the memory of those years. "Yeah. Only four years. Not like some kids stuck in child services all of their youth." She swallowed down the tightness in her throat as she recalled Amy and Emily. *Amy.* She jammed her eyes closed against the pain. Amy wasn't stuck in foster care anymore.

"What? What is it?"

Her stomach cramped, recalling the pain, the horror of Amy's death. "I came here last night looking for—" She stopped at the strangled, unrecognizable sound of her voice. "Looking for two girls—" She buried her face in her knees, freezing the burn of tears in her eyes, refusing to let them fall in front of this stranger, refusing to let her emotions out. Keep them in. Funny, considering all she ever did was fight to shove out the emotions of others.

"Let me guess. Dead." The coldness of his voice felt like an injection of ice in her veins. "They were dead the moment the pack had them in their sights. You should never have followed them here."

She shivered at his coldness. "They were my responsibility."

"Your mistake then, to ever let them leave your care and come here."

His words fueled her temper. And partly because she believed them. "How do you know so much about it? You don't appear to be doing that great yourself. If you're here, I'm guessing you screwed up somewhere along the way, too."

Who the hell was *he* anyway? Her jaw clenched. While she had disclosed a great deal about herself, she knew next to nothing about him. "Who are you? How did you land in here?"

Silence held for several minutes . . . and there was still that desperation humming in the cold air, strumming through her nerves. And underneath it, always danger.

His voice sounded hollow, wearied. "No. You talk to me. Tell me more about you."

"Can't I at least know your name?"

In the shadows, he shook his head. "It won't end there."

"Where are you from?"

His sigh floated on the air. After some moments, he answered. "I was born in Spain, but I don't live anywhere. I have apartments in Barcelona, Vienna, Dublin. No home really."

"Wow." His life sounded exciting. Completely opposite from hers. Travel. People. Adventure. "You must do well for yourself to live that way."

"Well enough."

"What do you do?"

He cleared his throat. "Little of this. Little of that. I work on different . . . assignments."

"Sounds interesting. Contract work?"

"You could say that."

"How'd you get here?

"Enough questions," he snapped.

Fingers squeezing around her calves, she demanded, "Why?"

"Trust me. You don't want to know me. I'm not the kind of guy sweet little Southern belles need to know." A thread of warning hung in his words. The dark rumble of his voice made her shiver, and she didn't doubt he was right. But what choice did she have? She was stuck here with him. She needed to get to know him so she would not feel so terribly alone in this nightmare.

For a while, neither of them spoke. Strange emotions stirred from him, reaching her across the distance. A gnawing ache that made her rub her own belly in hunger. "You're starving," she murmured.

He laughed a dry, broken sound. "You can tell that, huh?" He stretched his broad torso and held his arms wide, his skin flexing over ridged muscle and his flat, washboard belly. He looked a bit thin, with a lean ranginess that reminded her of a starved wolf. She winced at the comparison, remembering last night again. *Werewolves*. She wouldn't have believed it if she hadn't seen it herself.

"They don't feed you down here?"

"That's not part of their plan for me."

She tensed. It was the first time he owned up to knowing any specifics. "And what is their plan for you?"

Their gazes locked, clung. Instead of answering her, he asked, "Who will miss you, Ruby? A boyfriend back home?" His gaze flicked to her bare ring finger.

She fidgeted where she sat. "No one."

"No one? Come. I don't believe that." And again

she felt that spike of desperation, a jump in the room's temperature, a sudden blast of need from him. He needed to hear she had someone—a clan of family waiting eagerly for her return. His dark eyes glittered with light across the distance. A chill chased across her skin, puckering her flesh.

"Well. There's Adele. My best friend. She'll freak when I don't make my plane." That was putting it mildly. "She's supposed to pick me up at the airport." The redhead would probably be on the phone with the U.S. Consulate. Their meeting in a grocery store years ago had sprung an unlikely friendship. Somehow Adele had known, had recognized that Ruby needed a friend in a town fond of gossiping about that peculiar Deveraux girl. She ran the back of her hand against her nose, muffling her sniff. Adele would care if she went missing. No one else.

The moon sat higher. Silvery light streamed through the window, casting her companion in a chalky luster. Her gaze skimmed the muscled calves stretched out before him. Strange that she carried on a conversation with a naked man so calmly. But then it seemed unfair to feel any embarrassment over his lack of clothing. He couldn't help the situation.

"You look exhausted. Get some rest." He closed his eyes then, but she was sure he did not sleep.

She felt his alertness. Sensed it in waves on the

air. In the cording of muscles and sinew in the long stretch of his legs. The guy was built. Even half-starved.

She sensed his tightly coiled tension, his readiness.

Only what was he waiting to happen?

She must have slept after all.

Deep night swallowed the cell in its bleak maw. She rose from the cold ground, her palms pushing her up off the floor. Moonlight filtered into the room. Tiny motes and particles danced in the moon's glow. Silence hummed around her. A sudden noise scratched the air—a rough moan cut short, as if someone muffled it, bit back or swallowed the sound.

"Hello?" She rose to all fours. If she knew his name, she would have used it. He huddled in the far corner, a hunkered, shaking shape. Pain flowed from him into her, lancing as a fire-hot needle poking all over her body. She had no hope to block it. At this intensity, it broke past all her shields.

She started to shake from the force of it. Blood tickled inside her nostrils and she sniffed fiercely. "Are you okay?" Was this death she felt? God, please, don't let him be dying.

She crawled toward him, her voice gentle as she placed a trembling hand on his shoulder. The skin felt smooth, warm—hot beneath her fingers. "What can I do for—"

He turned, moving so quickly he was a blur in the shadowed cell, his eyes a gleaming flash. She crashed to her back on the floor, her head hitting with a painful smack. Hard male body surrounded her, naked flesh burning through her clothing.

She managed a choking sound.

"What are you doing? I told you to stay on your side of the room." His face dipped until his beard rasped against her cheek and neck, the hot whisper of his breath a warm mist against her flesh. "God, you smell sweet."

She shuddered, lungs contracting as his tongue swept over her throat in a deep, savoring lick.

She whimpered as though stung.

His presence, his *touch*, paralyzed her. Emotions bled into her, an unwelcome infusion she could not block, try as she might. The same black ravaging hunger she felt from the monsters last night consumed her. Which made no sense. He wasn't one of them. He couldn't be. He didn't possess their freakish eyes. The full moon had been in the sky for hours now and hadn't turned him into one of them. So why should he project their same dark hunger?

Why should she feel such fear?

He was starving. That must be it. She'd never felt

starvation before. Apparently it felt this dark. This . . . deadly.

Something else simmered inside him, too. Something more. She prodded carefully at the feeling. *Lust*. It matched that dark craving in its intensity. Frightening, but not as frightening as the dark, clawing hunger. She would do anything to escape that.

Anything.

The lust and the black hunger warred, struggling for dominance. The hunger nosed ahead, deepened, grew. She gasped, struggling for breath, staving off her complete descent into terror.

"Please," she pleaded. "Your name." If he just gave her his name, she would feel connected to him, not so terrified. Maybe she could beat down the hunger. Maybe she could reach *him*.

She turned her face into him, seeking. "Please." Lips on his cold skin, she whispered against his scratchy cheek, ignoring the slight softening inside her at the utter maleness swirling around her.

"You're hurting me." She tried to lift her arms to shove at the impenetrable wall of him, but his hands pinned them down on either side of her head.

"God, help me," he groaned, pressing his hardness against her belly in a deep grind. Again, *lust*.

"Oh!" Fresh panic flared to life inside her. And a spark of response. His pain, the agony of his hunger threatened to consume her . . . but this emotion, his desire made her purr and arch against him in shameful response.

He nudged her higher on the floor and forced apart her legs, fitting his hardness directly at the juncture of her thighs. He released one of her arms. Instead of shoving at him with her hand, beating him, scratching him, fighting him, she curled her fingers into a naked shoulder, hissing at the contact, at the sensation of smooth, male flesh . . . instantly infused with all his lust, all his need, all his dark *wanting*. For her.

Her breasts grew achy, tightening at the tips. He rubbed the head of himself against her in feverish strokes, her slacks the only barrier between them.

Her mouth opened wide against his bristly cheek. A sharp cry ripped from her throat at the friction, at the pressure between her thighs that wasn't enough, wasn't deep enough, hard enough, fast enough. She needed her pants off.

The lust was enough. Enough to block out all the ugly emotions that had swirled around her moments ago.

God help her, as his desire rose, the blackness receded, faded to nothing.

The lust rose, stronger. Hotter.

"Sebastian," he spat out, his cheek rippling against her lips as he spoke.

"What?" She felt drunk, addled in the head.

"My name . . . is Sebastian."

There. The personal connection she craved, needed, to not feel so afraid. She let the tip of her tongue taste him, lick his bristly jaw, desperate to chase the whiff of menacing emotions even farther away. Instinct drove her. Told her she needed to do this. Sliding her hand between them, she found his hard length. With a shuddering sigh, she wrapped her fingers around him. He seemed to grow even larger in her hand.

"You're playing with fire," he growled, his other hand sliding slowly down her arm, dragging over her bare flesh, sending shockwaves of pleasure through her.

"I know," she gasped, flexing her fingers over him and giving him a gentle squeeze. The gnawing ache in him receded, replaced with stark, unadulterated lust.

And she did know.

Deep down, at a basic level, she understood how she could let him touch her, how she could touch him like this—a man whose face she would not even recognize on the street.

Stoking his desires obliterated all those dark, soul-sucking emotions. Her survival led her to this.

Above all, Ruby had always been a survivor.

She couldn't stop from responding. Couldn't stop

him as his hand undid the drawstring at her waist and unzipped her pants. His pulsing need hit her like a sledgehammer, leaving her breathless . . . willing, an accomplice in an act her rational self opposed.

The back of his fingers brushed her belly. The touch spiked heat straight between her legs. *Pleasure. Need.* She hissed at the sensation, loving what he was doing. What he felt. What she felt. There was no distinction.

Desire like this—*for her*—had never rolled off any man before. If it had, she would not have been able to resist.

Just as she couldn't resist now.

"I'm sorry," he gasped as he leaned down and pulled off her pants in a single move. "I know you don't understand . . . but I can't stop. I have to have you. So beautiful, so clean." They hit the floor nearby. Cool air caressed her legs. Goosebumps puckered her flesh. She shook her head, beyond words.

Remorse mingled with his passion as his weight came over her again, the feel of his hard muscled legs a shock sliding against her own. Hot need drove him and spilled over into her, leaving her writhing and aching with need.

He swiped a thumb over her cheek. His dark voice rumbled through her, hitting every aroused nerve as he spoke. "This may be the only thing that saves you."

Strange words, but she knew them to be true, *felt* his conviction.

"Yes."

He ripped her panties off then, leaving her exposed. Vulnerable.

He wedged himself deep between her legs, hard hands falling on her hips, holding her still.

She widened her thighs for him, offering herself up, welcoming him inside her body as if she did this sort of thing all the time. As if the large hard press of him was normal, familiar.

She throbbed, the core of her wet with desire. For him. For this.

Love with a stranger. A man she didn't even know. *It's not supposed to happen like this . . .*

He slid strong arms beneath her back, lifting her closer, off the unforgiving ground as if he cared for her comfort. Her head came off the floor.

Then he was there, hard, large, shoving his way inside her, stretching her with his fullness. No gentleness—just swift, hot need in one driving thrust. *Relief. Ecstasy. Gratification.*

7

She was wet, eager, taking him into her body as a more experienced woman would. Only she was not experienced. Sharp pain shot through her as the fullness of him sank deeply, a throbbing burn buried between her thighs.

She shoved at his chest and arched against him even as she felt his exultation, his deep pleasure sinking inside her warmth. Those ripples of bliss washed over her, making it the strangest moment of her life . . . this pain mingling with intense pleasure.

"Sorry, sorry, so sorry," he muttered as he slid out of her and plunged back inside. If possible, she felt him even deeper. He groaned, the sound reverberating into her.

He dove a hand into her hair, holding her for him. His other hand rose to clutch her breast through her tank. "I can't stop . . . it has to be . . ."

She nodded, murmuring incoherently. His lips found hers, his mouth hot, devouring. Her inner muscles stretched, accommodating the size of him, accepting the pleasure-pain.

It has to be. Yes, yes, yes . . .

He moved again then, faster, each pump harder, more savage than the one before. He was a beast over her and it didn't scare her. It thrilled her. The hard sound of their bodies meeting as he thrust in and out inflamed her. She lifted her hands to his flexing biceps, nails digging as she hung on, clung. Soft gasps tore from her lips, whimpers that grew louder with each plunge of him inside her until she screamed her need.

He lowered his head, biting down on her breast through her tank, taking the tip inside his mouth. She arched, offering herself closer for his hungry mouth.

Her hips lifted in an instinctive move, heels digging into the ground, allowing him deeper penetration. On and on, he moved. Hard, grinding thrusts that drove her into the floor.

It should have horrified her. For twenty-six years she could never get close to a man and now she let this happen. Her hands slid down his taut, bare back, feeling every undulating muscle. He no longer felt cold. Warm muscle and sinew rippled beneath her palms.

His pleasure burned raw, deep, primitive, and she experienced every bit of it. She could not even decipher his pleasure from hers anymore. In this, they were one, joined. Maybe it was all his and she just borrowed it, claimed it for her own. She didn't give a damn.

Her body tensed, tightening like a wire stretched taut. She exploded deep within, quivering beneath him, but she had no time to soak up the sensation before another was on her. In fast succession, she came again. And then again.

Her own climaxes had not subsided before she was swept away on his own ride.

He groaned, the sound strange, more animal than man.

He moved faster then, ruthless as he pounded into her, his hands digging into her hips, raising her from the ground. She looked up into his face, his eyes. They changed for a second, brightened at the centers. Glowed like the moon itself outside their cell. Then his eyes closed. He shouted. The sound reverberated through his body and into hers.

She took his climax deep inside her, crying out

at the intensity, the savagery . . . ten times what her own climax had felt like. This was wild, brutal, unearthly . . . like soaring into the sky and leaving her body behind.

He fell over her, his hard length still buried inside her . . . filling her, pulsing, a reminder, evidence that couldn't be escaped.

She pressed at the muscled shoulders stretched above her, the skin slick against her palms. She sensed his utter, deep gratification. His sudden drowsiness. Safer than the dark killing hunger. Safer than the rampant lust that just swept her away.

"Please. Get off me," she murmured in a voice so soft and quiet she wasn't sure she had spoken aloud.

He rolled off her and she sat up, snatching her ruined panties. She used them to try and clean herself, refusing to look at him, too mortified.

Oh, God. Her hand shook as she worked. Not only had she let some stranger take her virginity on the floor of a basement cell—a prison—she had not even used protection. She had lost herself entirely. Tears burned her eyes. How could she have let another's emotions so rule her that she blocked out her own?

Because his emotions were stronger, overwhelming. Too tempting.

She nodded, dragging her khakis on. Everything about him was more intense. More powerful than anyone she had ever met—*felt*. She'd gone on dates where the guy entertained sexual feelings . . . it never made her jump into bed with him. Quite the opposite. Those feelings had always made her feel too self-conscious.

Adele was right. She wasn't ready for the world.

Maybe she never would be.

"Hey." His shadowed form sat up. "I'm sorry—"

"Leave me alone."

"You were a virgin—"

"Shut up," she bit out, hating the reminder of what she lost. All that she surrendered to him. Not that she ever could forget it. Still, she didn't need him saying it aloud. Scurrying to the far side of the room, away from him, she tucked her knees to her chest and tried not to notice the dull soreness between her legs. She still felt him there . . . the aching throb.

"Why didn't you say something before we—"

She laughed, the sound hollow and brittle. "There wasn't much time for talking, was there? And would it have stopped you?"

He moved, stood, a towering shadow. "No. I had to do it." His words were flat, without apology. "There was no other way."

She shook her head. "What's that supposed to mean?"

None of it made sense. Not this, not what they had done. Not him, not her. Not the damned werewolves who locked them in here. Nor the fact that, deep down, she wasn't sorry it happened either.

She breathed in, filling her lungs with stale air. At least the terror was gone. For now.

She opened her mouth, ready to ask him about that . . . about why she felt the same black tide of hunger from him as she did from those lycans, but she bit her lip, stopping herself, reluctant to remind him of the emotions that ruled him . . . that convinced her it was okay, necessary even, to stoke his lust. To enjoy it as her own.

He wasn't one of them. That was enough. She was alive. Only a deep sense of satiation hung on the air. For whatever reason, he no longer emitted the terrible gnawing ache and she wouldn't question why. She was just glad for it.

"You did want it to happen, right?" His question cracked the air. He prowled the space, his hands flexing at his sides, tension singing through his every pore. *Regret*. The sour taste of it coated her mouth.

She wanted to deny it, wound him. Wanted to insist that she hadn't wanted it, hadn't reveled at the sweet fullness of him inside her. She wanted to call him a bastard.

"It was . . . fine," was all she could manage to get out.

"Why did you let me—"

"I won't let you do it again," she broke in, her voice hard with defiance, unwilling to answer his question . . . that his own want and desire had swept her away. The last thing she would do was confess her ability to feel his emotions even better than her own. Everyone who ever knew what she was thought she was a freak, looked at her like she was some sort of witch. Besides, telling him she was an empath wouldn't change anything, anyway.

His voice reached her, deep and low as thunder in the distance. "I can't promise you that."

Her eyes flared wide at the words. Alarm knotted her shoulders. And a secret thrill. "You will. You will leave me alone. I'm telling you now I don't want to do . . ." she couldn't even say it. She settled for: "I don't want to do *that* again with you. Understand?" Desperation made her voice shrill. She wouldn't let herself get swept away by him again. "You'll promise me that right now."

"If I made that promise, I would only be lying." His deep voice rolled over. Like some kind of ancient aphrodisiac, she felt herself responding to the sound of it. Her nipples hardened against the cotton of her bra. She palmed one breast and felt the wetness from his mouth still there, soaking the cotton fabric, caressing the beaded peak.

"Bastard," she hissed, dropping her hand and curling it into a fist so tight her nails cut into her palm. Once she could excuse, forgive. Herself and him. But a second time . . . "I'll hate you."

For a long moment he said nothing. She followed his tall, wiry form as he moved to the far side of the room and sank down. He propped one arm over a bent knee before speaking, his voice cold, matter-of-fact. "I can live with that."

"What are you?" she demanded, wild emotion sweeping her. "What kind of man would—"

"It would be best for you to stop thinking of me as you would a typical man. I'm not like any man you've ever known."

She sucked in a breath, confused and wishing she could see his face in the gloomy cell, unable to believe that she had just invited this man inside her body, shared with him what she had shared with no one else. And he had as good as vowed to do it again. "You're right. Only a monster would take a woman against her will."

Hardly the truth. She expected him to challenge

the lie, but he laughed. The sound, disturbing and horrible, scraped her spine. "How right you are. You would do well to remember that."

A monster. She was closer to the truth than she realized.

But he would be a monster if needed. He could live with taking her again. And again. Whether she wanted it or not, he could do it again if he had to. If her death were the alternative, he would take that lesser evil on himself.

There'd been women. Plenty. Brief encounters where he took and gave little in return. He had little to give. He was a creature whose own mother afforded him little love. Only enough to stay her hand from slitting his throat. She taught him well just how contemptible a thing he was. Not a creature of God, but an unholy aberration. Not a man to live his life in a normal fashion. No home to speak of. No roots. No woman for him to take to bed, to heart, to live with each day . . . to live *for*. He was not a mortal man to live such an ordinary life. *A lucky life*.

Suddenly he remembered that lesson. Remembered why women like Ruby were not for him. He wasn't up for falling in love with a woman he would have to eventually bury.

Yet he still craved her, wanted to cross the cell and find her wet heat again. The odor of sex permeated the small space, mingling with the tantalizing aroma that was all her.

She was a cleansing balm to his soul. He wanted her again, wanted to have her until those memories were wiped forever clean. She could do that, he realized with a jolt. She had been sweeter than anyone to come before.

If he were honest with himself, he would want her whether the moon was high or not. She was a tempting package with her smooth skin and silky dark hair and eyes that glowed fire. Long limbs, ample curves—she was built like women used to be. Before they aspired to be runway thin. And she felt like paradise around his cock, snug and tight.

Yes. He could live with her hatred. What he couldn't live with was her death.

Even though his survival depended on killing her, he could never live with himself if that happened. He had lived over a hundred years without taking an *innocent* life. He wasn't going to start now. Especially not with someone like Ruby Deveraux. An innocent, strangely untouched.

At least, she had been. *A virgin.* He closed his eyes in a severe blink, hating that he had been the one to take that from her. To steal her innocence away.

He was already cursed to hell for taking her like any well-used whore. Opening his eyes, he grimaced, watching her curl into herself across the room, as far from him as she could get. The distance wouldn't matter. If he had to take her again in order to stave off the hunger, then he would.

Hardening his heart, he tore his gaze from Ruby, studying the moon's glow filtering through the room, understanding, perhaps for the first time, the frightening power behind the call of it. His mother had known, but he had denied its influence on him, arrogantly thinking himself stronger, better than the lycan dogs out there.

The moon would begin to wane tomorrow. Maybe then the beast would be easier to control and Ruby wouldn't be in as much danger. From him, anyway.

He snorted. *Right*. He dragged a hand through his short hair, his nails scraping his scalp.

He looked at the woman again. She was on her side now, her eyes closed but he knew she was still awake. Sensed it in her every breath. Her hair formed a dark puddle, shiny water in the night. He remembered tangling his hand through it and his fingers itched, eager for the feel again.

If, by some miracle, they got out of this alive, he would do her the favor of disappearing from her life and return to what he did best. His lip curled over his teeth.

He wasn't a lycan . . . but he wasn't human either. As a dovenatu, the moon might intensify his impulses, but he could shift at will—the main reason the pack so badly wanted him for their own. They would use him if they could convert him to their side. Their mistake was in underestimating what he would do to them when he broke free.

He'd have his vengeance.

Lycans had done this to him . . . to her.

An angry fire burned in his chest. Hunting them would never be sweeter.

8

Yusuf entered the room, Annika trailing one step behind him. Sebastian surged to his feet. His eyes fell on the tray of food Yusuf held. Warm bread. Savory, baked with herbs and spices, drizzled with olive oil. He could even smell the coolness of the water in the glass beside it. His mouth salivated.

"Down, boy. This isn't for you." Annika stood between him and Ruby, revealing her weapon. He inhaled deeply. Silver bullets. A subtle aroma, but he recognized it after packing the same kind of bullets for years.

Not lethal to him. But they didn't know that. An advantageous difference between him and his lycan brethren. They simply thought he lived—and died—by their rules. He had thought the same, too. Before his brother's wife, Kit, also a dovenatu, took a silver bullet and lived. Good information . . . and not anything he felt inclined to share with them. Let them think it would kill him.

"You're going to feed me?" Ruby looked hesitantly from the tray to Sebastian. "Why? Why me and not him?"

Yusuf blinked and lowered a hand to her head, smoothing his palm over the dark mess of her hair. She knocked his touch away. "You don't understand, do you? How remiss that Sebastian here failed to explain . . ."

"Shut up," Sebastian growled, tensing, waiting, bracing himself. Now she would know. Now she would understand and look at him with disgust. Hatred. His stomach knotted.

Yusuf's smile vanished like a wisp of smoke. "What's this?" Head cocked, he breathed in and moved from Ruby. Sebastian watched, feeling a little sick as he bent and picked up Ruby's torn and discarded panties. A sick thought came to him then. He was little better than the lycan who raped his mother. A rape that produced him and Rafe, sons she both loved and hated.

"Ah, Sebastian." Eyes glinting, Yusuf fisted them. "You beast. You didn't waste any time, did you?" He brought the underwear to his nose.

Sebastian watched Ruby shudder and press as tightly as possible against the wall.

"Ah, just as I thought. A virgin. Well, you used to be, at least." His laughter raised the hairs on Sebastian's arms and he leaned forward, ready to grab the gun from Annika and lodge a silver bullet in the bastard's chest.

The female lycan glared darkly at him, the gun aimed at his chest. Her lips curled in a sneer. "Guess we didn't tire you out enough if you still had appetite enough for her."

Yusuf crouched beside Ruby. "Was it so very bad, love? Tell Yusuf about it. Was he rough with your delicate body? Humans . . . you tear so easily." He dropped a hand on her shoulder and Sebastian surged forward. The barrel of Annika's gun directly in his face stopped him.

Holding still, he forced a deep breath into his lungs. *Steady*. They'll leave her be. They'd given her to him. Gunter wouldn't tolerate Yusuf toying with her. They wanted him to feed on her, after all. He stared down the barrel, hatred filling his heart.

Ruby shoved the hand off her. Yusuf lifted it again, ready to touch her, when Annika's voice stopped him. "Leave the bitch. Let her eat so we can go. I have other things to do."

With a grunt, Yusuf held out the tray to her. Shooting Sebastian an almost guilty glance, Ruby snatched the small loaf and began eating, her movements savage as she ate. Sebastian tried to look away—the sight of her teeth tearing into that bread was too much—but his eyes kept coming back to her.

Yusuf handed her the glass of water after she finished off the bread. She drank, watching the lycans closely over the rim. Finished, she set the cup back down on the tray and carefully wiped her mouth. "Why so concerned that I eat?"

The lycans exchanged looks, smiling. "You don't know anything, do you?" Annika shook her head. "This is really too delicious."

Sebastian clenched his hands, a low growl rising from his chest. They would tell her now. He couldn't stop them. No matter how much he wanted to.

His feet shuffled backward on the cold floor, sinking into the shadows as if distance would protect him from the coming revelation, from the look in her eyes when she learned the truth.

"We have to keep you alive and well so that our Sebastian here"—Annika's smile deepened, her lips an obscene stretch of glossy red as she paused for dramatic effect—"can feed on you."

Ruby blinked and stared at Sebastian for several moments, her eyes blank. She opened and closed her mouth several times as if preparing to speak. "That's impossible. He's not one of you. His eyes . . ." She motioned to his body where he lurked in the shadows.

"He did not change last night. It was a full moon. He's not a lycan. You're wrong." This last she uttered with absolute conviction. His disgust with himself twisted inside him, a dark, living serpent that he could not escape.

"You didn't think your lover boy here was some sort of prince, stuck in a dungeon with you? Is that why you let him fuck you?" Annika laughed then.

Sebastian's fingers curled into fists, yearning to strike.

Yusuf joined in her laughter. "More like a fire-breathing dragon with an appetite for damsels in distress." He wrapped an arm around Ruby and this time she did not even flinch from the unwanted closeness. Sebastian cursed beneath his breath. Why did she not speak? Move? No matter how she felt about him, she should care that a snake held her so close. Where was her self-preservation?

"Love," the lycan breathed near her ear. "He will feed . . . on you. He's brethren . . . even if a mongrel cousin. A dovenatu."

Her lips barely moved. "What's that?"

Yusuf's lips pulled into a cruel smile. "He's a half-breed. He can shift at will, not just during moon-rise, although the compulsion is certainly stronger then. Along with all other instincts." Yusuf lifted his head and called out cheerfully in his direction. "That right, Sebastian?" Turning back to Ruby, he continued, "And he doesn't have to feed, but starving as he is . . ." He clucked his tongue in mock sympathy. "Instinct, that part of him that's lycan, will demand it. That's where you'll come in, love."

She flinched. Those honey-brown eyes turned on Sebastian, burning into him with such horror, looking at him as if he were the same as they. A predator to be feared, reviled.

"Ruby," he said, but the sound of her name hung, suspended, and he could think of nothing else to say. What explanation could he give? He had spent a lifetime running from the beast. Hunting and killing as though that could change what he was. But the beast was there, inside him, ready to come out when survival demanded. Like now.

"Is it true?" she demanded.

He stared, unspeaking.

She charged forward—probably not the wisest course given what she had just learned. "Damn you. Don't stand there staring at me, feeling guilty about the fact that you're going to *kill* me! Eat me like some kind of m-monster." She choked on the last word.

He cocked his head to the side. There she went again. Reading his mind, his heart. It's like she was his damned conscience! How did she do that? Was he so transparent? He'd never thought so before.

"You never thought I had the right to know? And after we—we . . ." She couldn't manage the words. Her palm exploded across his face. He could have moved, could have dodged the blow, but he took it. Deserved it. For what he was. For fucking her . . . for what could happen if he didn't break them out of this cell.

The two lycans watched with avid interest the little drama they had orchestrated, silver eyes glittering.

It occurred to him that he might not get a better chance than now, while they were so distracted. And God knew his wrath needed an outlet.

Blood pumping, he whipped past Ruby and launched himself at Annika. They went down hard. The pistol flew from her hand and Sebastian dove after it. He wrapped a hand around it just as Ruby's scream shook the stale air and settled deep in the pit of his clawing gut. He glanced over his shoulder and froze.

Yusuf held Ruby before him, his pale hand stark and obscene against the flesh of her throat. Her eyes fixed on him, round and enormous. Pleading.

"Oh, Sebastian, Sebastian." Yusuf shook his head. "Points for trying. But do you really want to see her pretty neck ripped open?"

Sebastian started toward them.

Yusuf pulled Ruby's neck back from her shoulders in a deep arch. She whimpered, the tendons in her throat stretched tight. Sebastian stopped hard, feet sliding to a halt on the cold floor. It would take little effort for the lycan to decapitate her—Sebastian knew he was capable of such viciousness.

Chest tight, he rose slowly from his crouch. Annika stepped forward and plucked the gun from his fingers. It took all his will to stand strong. The hunger scraping the insides of his belly nearly brought him to his knees. He felt broken. Weak. Spent. Perhaps he needed to find a way to finish himself off . . . before he finished Ruby.

"All right now. Let her go," he growled.

Ruby whimpered again as the lycan pulled her tighter against his front. Her breasts strained against her tank, the full mounds riding the bastard's arm.

Yusuf smirked. "But she feels so good." The lycan inhaled the flesh of her neck. "And she smells so sweet . . . even with your stink on her." He dragged long-nailed fingers across her throat.

"Yusuf," Annika hissed in warning. "Don't. Gunter won't . . ." her voice faded at the quelling look her cohort sent her. Clearly Yusuf outranked her.

Sebastian angled his head and frowned, looking between the pair . . . realizing too late what it was Annika already saw coming.

"No!" He rushed forward just as Yusuf scratched her throat . . . not too deeply, just hard enough for three scratches to well with blood.

Sweet, intoxicating woman blood . . . earthy, already a hint spicy from the savory bread she had consumed, filled his nose.

With a groan, Yusuf lowered his head and licked her neck, his tongue nearly as dark as her wine-red blood that he lapped.

Straining to escape his mouth, Ruby cried out, the sound stark and desperate, clawing through Sebastian.

"No!" he shouted again, savage fury spiraling through him. But it was too late. The damage was done.

The lycan released her. She fell to the floor on all fours, her hair falling in a dark veil that covered her face.

Yusuf stepped over her. Chuckling, he and Annika took the tray and departed. The bolt fell into place, a loud clank as he sank down beside Ruby, afraid to touch her crumpled form. Afraid not to. His throat tightened with emotion. His hand hovered above her head.

She lifted her face, tossing back her hair, her brown eyes glowing embers that reached inside him. She splayed one hand against the bleeding scratches on her neck. "Shit," she muttered, shaking her head. Fresh blood kissed the press of her fingers, and the sweet aroma made him dizzy with need.

"Ruby," he breathed, the sound of her name brimming with pain and regret. Undoubtedly, she could hear it. Read it in his face.

"What?" Her wide-eyed gaze scanned him, quick as a moth flitting, searching for heat. "What?" she demanded, her voice growing shrill. "It's just a scratch." Her expression turned exasperated. "I'll admit his licking me was pretty gross, but it's no big deal." Her voice quavered. "I'll be fine. At least they're gone."

She didn't understand. And he needed to make her understand. "No. You won't be fine."

"What do you mean?"

"All it takes is a bite." He shrugged. "A lick. A scratch."

She fell still. "What are you saying?"

He angled his head, cutting his gaze into her meaningfully. "I think you get what I'm saying."

She pushed herself close to him. "No. I want to hear it. Say it. Explain it to me. No more omissions or lies."

He leveled a steady gaze on her, forcing all sentimentality, all emotion out. "You're one of them now. Or you will be. You'll begin transitioning in the next few hours. Maybe later." He nodded toward her neck. "The point of infection was small. A larger bite and transition would be immediate."

She pressed her palm against her temple, her voice a tormented whisper, as she closed her eyes. "This can't be. I'm going to wake up and this will all be a dream." Her voice grew into a faster rush. "I'll be back in Louisiana, in my own house, in my kitchen, there's a pot of gumbo on the stove, my tomato basil bread in the oven . . ." She shook her head harder, her voice a fevered rush. "I just want to go home."

"Ruby—"

"Guy Fieri's on TV and I'm diving for a pen to jot down his chow-chow recipe. I can see it. Smell home. *I'm there.*"

He closed his hands over her shoulders and gave her a little shake. "Ruby, stop it."

Her eyes burst open, glittering with tears. "No! Why should I? You just told me I'm going to turn into some damned werewolf!"

"There's a chance—"

"What? What chance?"

"We just have to kill Gunter. The pack's alpha. Before . . ."

"Before what?"

"Before you shift . . . and feed next moonrise. After that, your soul is lost. All hope of ever returning to normal will be gone after that."

She quivered in his hands and closed her eyes in a pained blink that he felt radiate through his dry and starved bones.

"Oh, God. Well. Since it sounds easy. Sure."

"We can do this." He nodded, even though his gut clenched at the avowal. How in the hell was he going to accomplish that when he couldn't break them free of this room? He could scarcely drag himself to stand.

Some of the angry fire died in her eyes, replaced with weary despair. "What are you talking about?" She shrugged free of his hands. "You're not going to help me. According to Yusuf, you won't last that long before you break down and—and—"

"I won't," he vowed, even though he doubted the truth of his own words. How could he make such a promise when he had never been in a fix like this before, when he just didn't know . . .

He tried to touch her again, his hand reaching for hers. She moved it quickly, tucking both hands behind her before he could make contact. Of course, she wouldn't want his touch. In her eyes, he was no better than Yusuf.

"You can't make that promise. You can't know that you won't attack me."

She spoke the truth. In this condition, starving . . . who knew what he would do? He'd always been so careful to never find out. Had he been mortal, he would have already died from lack of food and water. The only thing keeping him alive was that he was a dovenatu. The beast kept him alive . . . and the beast couldn't continue much longer without food.

"Let's just go back to our opposite walls," she suggested, nodding at what he had come to think of as *her* wall. "Don't talk to me. Don't look at me. And damn it, don't touch me."

Settling against the wall, she drew her knees up to her chest in that protective pose again.

He studied her a moment before walking across the room in silent strides. His body so cold. Bloodless. Starving.

He felt her stare following him, boring into his naked back. At the wall, he turned and met her gaze, noting the shimmer of doubt there . . . the fear that had lurked from the start.

He wondered if there would ever come a day when he did not see fear in her eyes. If so, he doubted he would be around to see it.

Soon he'd be free. Out in the world again.

Hunting the likes of her.

Maybe an hour passed since she had been infected. Maybe more. Hours. Days. Time blurred since she'd been tossed down in this dungeon. She'd had enough time to think, time for questions to start filling her head.

"Are you going to explain to me what you are? Exactly?"

He opened his eyes and fixed them on her across the cell.

To fill the strained silence, she added, "There's not a lot else to do as I wait to turn into a werewolf, is there?" The sarcastic edge faded from her voice as she whispered, "Make me understand this. I need to understand."

"What do you want to know?"

"How did you become a dovenatu? Why do they want you so much?"

He sighed. "I was born this way, transitioned when I was fourteen. Me and my twin brother. I can shift at will. Not just during moonrise."

"And that's why they want you so badly?"

"I'm stronger than a lycan. Unless it's moonrise, then the playing field is pretty even. But one-on-one, when the moon isn't full, there's little contest. I can shift. They can't. They're only at their strongest during full shift."

"So, you're quite a prize for them."

"If they can recruit me."

Which they planned on doing. Through using her. Her throat thickened.

"They won't," he vowed. "I don't have to feed, don't have to kill."

"Unless you're starving," she injected, the bitterness back.

The first man she had given herself to would be the death of her. But he was more than that. He was the first man she had ever felt anything for. Suddenly the thought of him, over her, *inside* her, filled her head. The stark pleasure, the need he drew deep inside her, made her quiver. She moistened, dry lips had rubbed at her chest, over the throbbing ache beneath her breastbone that kicked in at the very idea of him killing her.

"I've hunted lycans since I left home at seventeen. I hunt them down like dogs and kill them. As far as I'm concerned they need to be wiped from the earth."

She swallowed. *He was talking about her.* Did he realize that? At least she knew where they stood if they didn't kill Gunter and break her curse. "Big job for one man."

"There are others. Organizations of hunters. Both in Europe and the States. And don't forget I'm blessed with long life." His lips twisted as though this were not necessarily a blessing. "I've killed many lycans. And I'll kill more yet. Once I get out of here."

Eager to change the subject from his dedication to killing lycans . . . killing the likes of her, she asked, "Were your parents like you? Dovenatus?"

"No. As far as I know, there aren't many of us. My brother. His wife. I know of no others. That's not to say they're not out there. Blending in. Suppressing the part of them that's more beast than human."

"If your parents aren't dovenatus, then how did you—"

"My mother descends from Etienne Marshan . . .

before a witch cursed him into the world's first lycan. Meaning that my mother descended from the son born to him before he was cursed. Lycans cannot procreate with humans. Different species and all that. But a Marshan descendant like my mother shares compatible DNA with lycans. Meaning she can breed with a lycan where humans cannot."

"So your mother slept with a lycan?"

"A lycan raped my mother. And my brother and I are the result. Dovenatus."

"Oh." Her voice rang with reproach. "So you've got the lucky side of the gene pool. All the perks and none of the disadvantages."

His eyes glittered across the distance, bright flames twisting at the centers. "I guess. Only I don't feel very lucky right now."

"No?" she snapped. "Well, neither do I. I'm sorry if I don't extend you my sympathy. I'm reserving it for myself."

"I didn't get you in this," he reminded. "You stuck your nose where it didn't belong."

She sprang to her feet and approached him in a furious stalk, forgetting about keeping to her side of the room. "So this is all *my* fault?"

"If I were you, little girl," he growled, lifting a finger, "I'd take myself back over there."

She stopped, looking down at him where he sat,

utterly still, legs stretched before him in a deceptively reposed position. His eerie gaze traveled the length of her, and she felt the desire that was becoming so familiar. Addictive heat pooled low in her belly, and she was swamped with the memory of his body locked with hers.

She shook her head, her hair brushing her cheek. That couldn't be ordinary. Couldn't be just because he was a dovenatu. This chemistry had to be him. *Her.* Her breasts tightened, tingled against her top, and she knew she wanted him again. If he made the slightest move, gave her the slightest sign, she'd fall on him, greedy for more.

Then his gaze shifted, stopping to rest on her neck where Yusuf had scratched her. Her fingers flew there, brushing the gritty, dried blood.

Hunger. It slammed into her, the bleak ache clawed her in a savage swipe that nearly bowed her over.

Reminded of the predator he was, she quickly retreated, tossing up her barriers, doing her best to guard herself from the deadly beast that lurked so close. She shoved back the tender thoughts she'd harbored for him, her first lover—the consuming desire.

She couldn't let that blind her to what he was, to the very real danger he posed. Sinking to the floor, she drew her knees close, closed her eyes and thought of home.

9

Two days passed and still she slept. He knew it was the way with every newly infected lycan, just as was the fever raging through her. He knew she was senseless to the world—to his presence—and he was glad for that small favor. He moved from the corner where he had tracked a trickle of water and lapped what he could from the wall. Settling down on the floor, he propped a hand on his bent knee and watched her. In the deep silence of her sleep, he could almost pretend she wasn't there. Almost.

Sitting on his side of the cell, bitter cold, his blood a slow chug in his starved, constricting veins, he fought down sympathy for her. What would be the point? He never sympathized for his prey before.

He killed them. And she was prey now. A lycan. His enemy. It didn't matter that the scent of her was buried on his soul. That he craved her. That he wanted her again. That he would likely never forget the shattering release he found in her body.

Through the darkness, he scanned the curve of her neck. The blood had long dried to a rusty brown on the creamy flesh. His mouth salivated.

Killing her would be justified. His conscience could accept it—*should*. As soon as the idea entered his head he shoved it down with a savage curse. No. Never.

His gaze devoured her, drinking in the curve of her jaw, the full lips, the nose that tilted slightly up at the end. With her eyes shut, he saw her eyes as he remembered them. The fiery gold-brown that melted anyone who looked into them—the memory of those eyes warmed him when he felt only the bitter cold in his bones.

He couldn't kill her. Even though he desperately craved food, nourishment, *life*. He couldn't.

Not when he craved her more.

Ruby dreamed of hell.

It must be hell. Amy chased her through a forest of fog. Branches and brambles clawed her, tearing her clothes, her skin. Only it wasn't Amy. Not really.

Not anymore. The monster with blood-stained teeth stretched her gore-covered talons for Ruby, flexing on dense air.

Ruby ran harder, faster, legs pumping through yellowed fog. Her breath fell quick and hard, filling her ears like the endless buzzing of a clock. Ahead she spotted her house with the giant cypress tree draped beside it. Curtains of moss hung from the branches and drifted in the breeze. *Yes, yes, yes.*

If she just reached it, if she just made it inside . . .

Heat flared in her back, needle-lancing pain that spread outward. She toppled down with a sharp cry. Flipping over, she fought, arching, hissing and scratching at her attacker—the beast that would have her if she did not fight, if she did not resist. She lashed out, striking, hitting. Her fists connected with something hard.

"Ruby! Ruby!"

Her eyes flew open. She gulped down stale air and focused on the shadowy figure above her. The sharp lines and gaunt planes of a man's face blurred in and out before her.

"Ruby, settle down. Don't fight it. You're making it worse."

"Sebastian," she breathed heavily, as if having run a great distance and reached the end, the finish line.

She took a quick glance around their fogless space.

She was still stuck in the cell, nowhere near her home. Nowhere near Amy, beast or not. The girl was dead. Despite Ruby's promise to help her. She brushed a hand against her cheek, wincing at her fiery flesh and the wetness that could only be tears. The pain in her back came again. It burned through her, radiating throughout her entire body. She moaned, arms clutching at her middle.

"What's happening to me?"

"You're transitioning."

She shook her head, not understanding, her brain felt thick, thoughts sluggish, like the drip of syrup from a spout.

He pulled her into her arms, holding her tightly. And she let him, clung to him, listened to the hard thump of his heart against her ear. *Not a monster. Not a monster.* He couldn't be . . . she wouldn't have done what she did with a monster, wouldn't relish the hard press of his body, a predator who would devour her . . .

Shudders shook her. She moaned, fighting his embrace.

Sympathy. It felt good. The arms strong, supportive.

He hugged her tighter, compassion rolling off him and into her. She stopped fighting. His heartbeat sounded louder against her ear. "Don't fight it, Ruby. Don't resist. It will go easier for you."

"I don't understand." She turned her face, her lips

brushing his chest as she spoke. With a will of its own, her tongue darted out to taste salty skin. Her eyes burned, tears pricking at the corners and she clung to him tighter, pressed her body closer, moaned at the sudden needy clench of her belly.

He gasped, his arms squeezing her back, tightening even more around her. A shot of desire trickled through the awful, aching burn of hunger dwelling inside him. *Liquid-hot want.*

She latched onto it, her fingers digging into his arms, clinging. "Yes," she growled. "Take me. Please. Again."

Then his desire faded. The flame dimming, dying. For the arrival of a new emotion.

Sour regret. Heavy grief.

He gripped her arms. Dragged her away from him.

She shook her head, hair tossing, catching in her mouth.

"You don't really want that. You just want to escape the—" He stopped and she knew he was trying to think of a way to make the truth sound better— not so bad. She got that, but she wouldn't accept it. She had to know what was happening. Why he felt so sorry for her.

"What? Tell me," she gritted through teeth clenched tight against the sweep of tearing heat in her bones and muscles . . . incinerating pain.

"Your death."

Her belly cramped, the terrible sensation reminiscent of other times. Sometimes she accidentally flipped to a news station when the horrific footage of a shooting flashed across the screen, zooming in on a victim writhing pain. But then she could flip the channel and sever the connection before her nose started gushing blood.

She couldn't flip the channel right now. She could only endure. A deep keening moan poured from her lips.

This time the pain was her own. The death she felt hers.

Her lids drifted shut. Blackness rolled in.

Sebastian flexed his hands and eased them off Ruby, even though the heat of her skin felt good—*she* felt good. Warming to his cold, cold flesh. But he couldn't let himself touch her any longer. Not with his own agony ripping through him. Not with her words ringing in his ears. *Take me.* It had killed him not to oblige, not to sink into her softness and forget where they were.

Knowing he had to, he lowered her back down and dragged himself to his side of the cell. Away from her. His gaze fixed on her where she curled into a small ball. Even mindless with the fever, her human DNA dying, making room for the new, his pulse leapt at the sight of her. His cock hardened in the chill air, remembering the warmth of her tightness.

During transition, she was weak, feverish, vulnerable. *Willing*. It would be so easy . . .

He cursed and dragged a hand over his face, shoving down the base, dark instincts at war inside him. He couldn't do that. The one time had been bad enough. But even as he told himself this, he knew he might have to. A lycan fed and fucked. Not always in that order. Right now, he was operating at their level. His state of starvation blinded him to all his long-held principles. To the humanity and morals pounded in him by his mother, and then his brother—a far better man than he.

He fully intended to survive this. To kill Gunter. And Yusuf. All of them. The entire pack. With great and slow pleasure. And then Ruby would be all right. Her curse would be broken. She would be human again. He would make all this up to her.

Make it up to her? He dropped his head back to beat against the wall.

Where the hell had that sentiment come from? His life wasn't one of sentimentality. There was no room in it for anything besides hunting down the bastards like the ones upstairs. That hadn't changed. There wasn't room in his world for her.

He wasn't like his brother. He didn't go for missions of mercy. Didn't get married and do the whole domestic thing. He hadn't lost so much of himself that he didn't remember who he was. And who he would be again when all of this was over.

Who Ruby Deveraux was would fail to matter to him then. It had to.

The sound of the door scraping open woke her.

She lifted herself on limbs that felt surprisingly light and limber given her cotton-stuffed head. Holding a hand against her eyes, she blinked against the light flooding the room through the door, limning several large figures. *Lycans.*

She tensed at their arrival, at the strange emptiness they emitted. Now she could identify that bleak gray she felt. *Evil.* Noxious as toxic gas.

She pressed fingers to her lips, as if that would stop the rising tide of bile in her throat. She felt sick from it—*them*—and sicker yet when she remembered she was one of them now. A lycan that would feed on the next moonrise.

"Sebastian," she murmured, even as she resented that she should call out to him, that she had come to rely on him. Need him so much. Her lifeline in this frightening new world. Her gaze found him, already standing across from her, his body poised and ready, taut as wire worked tight.

Then she felt him. *Rage. Killing fury.* Dark suspicion radiated from him.

His palms pressed flat against the stone wall as though he might use it for leverage and spring at any moment. His naked body was whipcord-lean, reminding her of a hungry jungle cat. Whatever they had in store for them, he would fight it.

"Disappointing." Gunter and the others surveyed them with gleaming eyes. Sighing, the alpha strolled deeper inside the room with his hands clasped behind him. "We've trouble coming. We've lost contact with our allies to the west. I haven't the time or patience for this anymore. If you're with us or not, let it be decided now."

"I'm not."

Her chest swelled with relief, her heart clenching with emotion. He meant it. She knew . . . *felt* that he spoke the truth. He would die first before killing her.

Gunter cocked his head. "Strange. You hunt and kill lycans." He waved a hand at Ruby. "Precisely what she now is. Yet you would choose your own death over hers."

Her eyes locked on his across the distance, her

vision faultless. She saw the light twisting at the centers of his eyes. His voice fell hard. *Angry.* "It's what it will do to me. Turn me into one of you fuckers," he bit out. Ruby flinched. Of course. It had nothing to do with her. He cared nothing for her. He didn't want to be like them. *Her.*

Time suspended. No one spoke, moved, breathed.

Without turning her head, Ruby's gaze shifted to stare at Sebastian, the tight set of his lips in his unshaven face, afraid to be the one to upset the eerie stalemate.

Gunter's thick accents cracked the silence. "Hold her."

Ruby shot to her feet just as they came at her. She tried to break past. Impossible. A lycan flung her back. She struck the wall with bone-jarring force. Stunned, she lolled there, the air left her body in a rush of wind.

Sebastian lunged off his wall with a sound more animal than man. Three lycans fell on him, holding him back. Restrained, he watched as Yusuf caught her up in his arms and forced her before Gunter. She felt like a helpless kitten in the lycan's paws.

The alpha squared off in front of her, unsheathing a fierce-looking knife, the blade glinting like their eyes when caught in light.

"It won't kill you, but it will hurt." He shook his head, as though apologetic over that fact. With a nod at Sebastian, he added, "But there'll be lots of blood. Precisely what's needed to get our friend to behave as he ought and stop being so reticent." The alpha's mouth thinned into a tight line, his gaze sliding over her in consideration.

It dawned on her then. Cold horror washed over her.

He was deciding where to cut.

"No!" She struggled against the hard hands clamped on her arms.

Gunter slid a step closer, holding the blade oddly before him, turning it sideways as though taking measure. "Sssh. Don't struggle," he murmured, his free hand grabbing a fistful of her hair.

She fought, kicking in a frenzy. She felt several strands rip from her head, but she still could not break free.

"He's turning!" shouted one of the lycans holding Sebastian.

Ruby stilled, tearing her gaze from the blade's mesmerizing gleam to watch. Fresh horror filled her as Sebastian twisted and writhed, his skin pulling and . . . expanding. He hunkered at the waist, his back curving deeply as he bent, turning into the very thing they wanted to use and manipulate so badly.

Gunter exhaled, the sound reverent, satisfied. "Yes. That's it."

Sebastian unfolded into a standing position, throwing the other lycans off him. She forgot about the painful grip on her hair, about Yusuf's hard hands on her, about the blade pointing in her direction.

She could only stare at Sebastian. Her eyes felt enormous, dry and unblinking in her face, as she drank in the sight of him, similar to the monstrous lycans, but with sleeker lines, less hair. Muscle and sinew rippled his large frame.

"Yes," she echoed, as he broke through the lycans rising up to take him.

Cool purpose flowed from him; the only anger she felt was controlled, directed at their captors. Not her.

Relief rolled through her. He wasn't like them. He would help her, would stop them—

Pain. Searing force drove deep into her stomach, burning upward through her chest and throat—fire and agony. She opened her mouth on a scream that never came. Blood filled her mouth. Her nose. Choked her.

She hunched forward against the terrible pressure, gagging and coughing, blood spattering from her lips, fingers digging into the arm that seemed connected to her body, to the handle of a knife buried deep in her. There was a grinding scrape of blade against her bone.

The hands on her arms loosened, dropping away. She staggered forward, clung to Gunter, clutching him in a parody of a hug, her mouth wide in a silent cry. Blood gurgled at the back of her throat.

Just when she thought the pain couldn't get worse, Gunter buried the blade deeper, sliding it higher, ripping upward. Her body jerked. Tears blurred her vision as her body convulsed, dying.

Gunter slid the blade free from her body. His voice sounded far away, as if he called from under water. "Resist her now, dog."

He vanished, moving toward the door in a blur. She fell to the ground, rolling onto her back.

Sebastian arrived, dropping heavily beside her.

The bolt slid home, the loud clank reverberating over her harsh breath, each inhalation slowed, slowing, then stilling.

Was she dead? Cold swept through her. Emptiness. No more pain, at least. Just a strange peace. Ease.

Blood covered her, sputtering from her lips as she tried to speak. The metallic odor filled her nose.

Sebastian leaned over her. She stared up into his horribly beautiful face, a creature of nightmares, skin a gleaming bronze where hair did not cover. His lips parted, peeling back from his teeth. Fingers like talons gripped her arms and pulled her toward him.

As his face neared, descending, she let loose a choked sob. This was it. They had broken him. He would have her now.

10

His touch returned her to the pain. To living agony. It forced her head up off the ground with a shrill cry.

Agony drowned him, swimming with the frothing fury and hunger. It pressed down on her like a great, heavy blanket from which she could not escape. His hard hands flexed around her arms and she hissed, tossing her head. Sebastian stared from her face to her stomach . . . to the open, blood-gushing wound there.

It was a strange thing smelling one's own blood. So much blood. She remembered Gunter's words. His assurance that this wouldn't kill her. Only it would. The wound spilled too much blood . . . the sight, the scent, the copious amount would break the last of Sebatian's will.

Clawing hunger ripped through him. *Torment.* She gasped, struggling against it. She couldn't take it, couldn't stand it another moment . . .

With every effort left to her, she brushed a hand against his cold cheek and managed to speak. "Make it stop."

At least the suffering would end. Ending it for him would end it for her.

"Go ahead!" The growl of her voice startled her, reminded her that she wasn't herself anymore—just some monster that the world needed to be rid of.

At least Sebastian would not die. The thought comforted her more than she would have thought possible. Better that she had known him. Tasted desire with him. *Through* him. She could have died with Amy and Emily and not known. Instead, she had had this time with him. For maybe the first time, she had well and truly lived.

A stark, unwelcome realization struck him, sinking through the deluge of dark, twisting hunger. She *wanted* him to kill her, to feed on her. His anger rose so swiftly, so furiously, it actually beat out the sweet scent of her blood, the temptation that threatened to consume him.

"Damn you, Ruby," he bit out, shaking her fiercely.

"Talk to me. I need to know you. Tell me who you are." It was the only way.

Her eyes stared up at him, confused, glazed, lost.

Damn her. He couldn't believe she was giving him permission to *feed* on her. *The hell he would!*

"What are you, Ruby?" He shook her. "There's more to you. Tell me. I need to know." He wet his cracked lips, avoiding looking down at all that blood again. Delicious moisture for his tight, parched arteries. He avoided breathing, avoided taking in the aroma that tormented his starved body.

"No," her voice rasped.

"Yes. I knew it the moment I saw you. You're . . . different. Special." A part of him suspected it was why he'd been able to resist her. She was no ordinary girl.

She laughed then. The dry, brittle sound like crackling leaves on the air. Without humor. Dark. Tormented. "Sure. Why not? It doesn't matter anymore." Her head lolled on her shoulders and she smiled a silly, drunken grin.

"C'mon. Give me something. A reason." A reason not to kill you. *A reason to believe you're as important as I think you are. Give me the strength to fight the darkness . . .*

She groaned. The sound tore through him. "I thought I couldn't be any weirder than I was. A freak my family didn't even want. And now this." She paused before saying. "I'm an empath."

He thought for a moment, struggling to think as he held down the beast, keeping it pinned. "You mean you know what others are feeling?"

She laughed that awful laugh again, her eyes fixing on him, glittering cold silver. She looked a bit more lucid. Regenerated. He didn't dare look at the wound to verify this. The blood would still be there, pushing at the fine edge of his will.

"I *know* what others are feeling because I feel it. I live it." Her voice dropped to a mutter. "I can't stop it."

"Christ." What hell must she have been through?

He nearly dropped his hands from her, afraid at all she must feel through him . . . his torment, the hunger. She must think him a monster. She must *know*. Her uncanny awareness made sense now.

This woman possessed power. People weren't always truthful . . . even with themselves. Mostly with themselves. They may not think certain thoughts . . . but the sentiment, the emotion was always there. That couldn't be denied. She could look inside the heart of anyone and see what hid there. He'd felt she was special. Now he knew.

Burning determination filled him. He would destroy himself before he destroyed her. His mouth curled in a savage smile. Releasing her, he moved back to the far wall. Away from her. Away from temptation.

She watched him, her pewter eyes eerie in an entirely different way—different from the lycans he hunted. Different because he cared about her.

"Sebastian?" she whispered.

He said nothing, not trusting himself to speak. Closing his eyes, he fought to feel nothing. To empty himself of everything. To spare her and let her heal.

11

He turned from her. Like everyone else before. *Like her father.*

She closed her eyes against the burning sting of tears. Great. She felt like a little girl again, crying when her dad turned his back on her, left her because he just couldn't handle what she was.

Merely another reminder of why she should have stayed home. The world waited with pain for anyone who dared live in it. She had known that. So why had she left her safe haven?

She peered at him through the darkness, the muscled hulk of him, a brooding shadow in his corner, half-man, half-animal. She should feel threatened, in danger. Instead, she only felt hurt. Unaccountably hurt that when she finally bared herself, revealed herself for what she was, he turned away.

She thought that maybe on some level he would understand. Because he was different, too.

Because she let him in her head . . . in her body.

But he didn't understand. Didn't forgive. Like everyone else.

Ruby shivered, even though she was starting to feel warm again. Healed. Only her heart ached. Stupidly. Why should she care what he thought of her? Why should she care about him at all?

She shouldn't.

But she did. She did, or she wouldn't hurt this much.

The ground shook above them. Ruby opened her eyes from a fitful sleep, alert to Sebastian's every sound and movement several feet away. He didn't stir, hardly breathed. *Hunger.* Craving smoldered inside him, held tightly in check, and she shivered.

He had not spoken to her since she made her confession. Not looked at her, did not touch her.

She had lost track of time, sleeping throughout her body's regeneration. She knew days had passed since she had been stabbed, but she hadn't a clue how many. At one point, they fed her, lycans standing guard between her and Sebastian. She had gulped down food without tasting, inhaling it, letting it fuel her.

The sounds from above grew, shaking on the air.

"What is it?" she whispered, watching as Sebastian rose to his feet. Primal as any wild animal even when he appeared human. Raw and menacing. Desperate for food. Life.

She eyed the gaunt press of his ribs against his sinewy body and felt the familiar pull. Desire that was all hers. The flexing of muscles in his satiny chest. He gazed up at the ceiling. Every muscle stretched taut as he balanced on the pads of his feet, looking upward as though he could see what went on above.

"It's begun."

"What?"

He cocked his head, listening. She could hear the sounds, too. Cries, sudden vibrating movements throughout the building. The faint, creeping odor of blood sifted through the air like growing smoke.

The image of that room from that first night with its buffet and free-flowing wine flashed through her head. Followed, of course, with the gorging beasts, the blood, the screams. *Pain. Ripping agony.*

"Are they feeding again?" she whispered, swallowing.

"It doesn't work like that. They can't do that right now. Not until the next moonrise."

"Then . . . what is it?"

"They're being attacked. By outsiders." His head cocked deeper to the side and he sniffed the air, so much resembling an animal just then that a chill chased down her spine. "A rival pack, I'm guessing. The one they've been worrying over."

"What does that mean for us? Is that bad?"

He frowned and she wondered if it was her question or the *us* that made him frown.

"Packs are territorial, but I've not heard of them making outright war on each other. Not in generations." In the shadowed cell, his lips twisted. "They've grown too civilized for that and don't encroach on each other. Unless . . ."

"Unless what?"

His gaze found hers, glittering across the distance like an animal peering out from the brush on a dark night. Light glowed and twisted at the centers like flame.

One of her many foster families had hunted, relying on game for most of their meat. Not uncommon in their corner of Louisiana. So Ruby knew how to hunt, lay a trap, skin and gut a kill. She also recognized the eyes of an animal watching her. Only before it had always been prey. Frightened. Hiding.

He was no one's prey.

"Unless," he answered, "the rumors of packs allying themselves and forming a confederation are true. They've grown sick of organized hunters, of NO-DEAL and EFLA."

She shook her head. She'd just learned of the existence of preternatural creatures—*had become one*—and now he was discussing things like lycan confederations and organizations of hunters. "Why are they doing that?"

"In order to unite, to let mankind know of their existence, defeat the hunters . . . and then take on the rest of the world."

Hot and cold intermittently washed over her at this. She opened her mouth with another question when he waved a hand. "Silence. Someone's coming."

Her heart picked up speed. "What do we—"

"Stay there." He sprang into the air like a jungle creature.

The door swung open and she held her breath, commanding her eyes to stay trained on the door, to *not* glance up where Sebastian hugged the ceiling like some sort of spider.

"You're still alive."

Yusuf. Even if his face and figure were cast in shadow, she knew his voice in an instant. Her nostrils flared. She even knew his smell. Sweat and bad cologne.

Behind him, Annika and another female hovered,

shifting anxiously. "Hurry. Grab him. He may be the only thing to keep them from killing us." Anxiety hummed from them as they rushed the room. And something else. Bitter and acrid, it filled her mouth, coating her tongue. *Fear.* They were afraid. *Panicky-hot.* But not from anything they faced in this room. They feared what they fled, whatever tangled with the rest of their pack above. Whatever waited Ruby and Sebastian if they got out of this room.

Yusuf's gaze flew wildly over the room, skipping over her, searching for Sebastian.

Noise descended on them. A terrible boom. Several violent thumps came closer. Shouts and crashes. A shrill scream.

Yusuf dragged her to her feet, gripping a fistful of her hair. "Where is he?"

She shook, words strangling on her lips, wincing at the grip on her head.

A shadow fell, swooped down.

Yusuf looked up the precise moment Sebastian dropped on him.

Ruby stumbled free as the two locked, a tangle of flying limbs and pummeling fists. The females plunged into the fray with ear-burning screeches, pouncing like cats on Sebastian.

"Go!" Sebastian shouted. "Run, Ruby! Run!"

The door loomed ahead. Open and clear, she dove

for it, intent on reaching the floor level, the front door. Escape. She only had to make it through warring lycans. No sweat. Right.

A niggle of guilt wormed through her. She paused, her heart a hammering thud in her chest. Glancing over her shoulder, she bit her lip. *Sebastian.* Her heart squeezed. She could still hear them—the smacking of fists on bodies—Sebastian's and Yusef's growls and grunts. Turning back, she faced the shadowed stairwell, the light ahead. Perspiration trickled down her nape.

Go. Run. You can't help him even if you tried.

A mantra grew in her head. *Get away. Get away. Get away.*

Exhaling, she rushed ahead, took the steps two at a time.

But he kept you alive, Ruby. You know what it cost him to do that, what he endured. You know because you felt it yourself.

Swallowing a sob, she shook her head. If she stayed around him, he would break—feed on her and become one of them. He was better off without her. They were both better off without each other. No matter how her heart ached. She forced the heartache away.

She didn't owe anything to a half-breed lycan who took her virginity . . . who made her body catch fire with a single touch. That sped up her strides and tightened her jaw. *Get a grip, Ruby. This is about survival. Your safety. Not about some guy making you go weak at the knees.*

No one met her at the top of the narrow stairs. She crept down an empty corridor, pressing close to one wall, palms skimming the smooth plaster. An eerie quiet prevailed, sending the small hairs along her arms into salute. *What happened to all the noise? The screams?*

Acutely aware of her aloneness, she paused, waiting for some sort of sound. Linked to her brethren, she felt Gunter and others nearby. So Gunter wasn't dead then. Unfortunate. If the alpha were dead, then she would be normal again. Free.

Closing her eyes, she reached inside herself and used her newly heightened senses. Over the beating of her heart, over the blood rushing in her veins, she heard a man speaking. The distant voice grew, gaining clarity. She cocked her head, listening, trying to detect his location. She followed the voice. Down the corridor. To the left.

She stopped at the corner, listening intently to the voice. She had never heard this man before. Never *felt* anything like him. *Immense cold.* Even in a language she did not understand, its rumble was different than that of Gunter, yet he spoke with such command that she knew he was an alpha.

She continued, rounding around the corner. The sound of the voice grew, but she saw no one. She stopped at a set of swinging double doors. Where death reeked. The voice came from within.

A covert look through one filth-covered window revealed a large room. Bodies sprawled between long-neglected machinery. Dead bodies. Pools of blood stained the cement floor. Her nostrils quivered against the coppery tang of it, something dark unfurling in her belly.

Her gaze landed on Gunter. He stood before a mob of at least fifty, mostly men, some women, all outfitted with weapons and dressed in brown fatigues. Warriors. Soldiers. Even through the grimy glass, she could see the pewter gleam in their eyes.

A dozen lycans hung behind Gunter, all that remained of his pack. And her, of course. Gunter lowered himself to his knees at the feet of a tall, fair-haired man standing at the helm of the invading mob.

The guy looked more like a rock star in his tight brown pants and a mesh top. A stunning redhead stood beside him, dressed as though she were attending a garden party in her silk halter dress. She seemed bored and untouched by the carnage around her. Her gaze flicked over Gunter's bowed head, clearly uninterested in his display of surrender.

Just then the female's gaze locked on Ruby through the dirt-splattered glass. Her lips parted. Words fell from her lips. She pointed a finger in Ruby's direction, and all heads swiveled to catch sight of her peeking in at them.

She fled. Her arms and legs pumped hard as she headed down the corridor, praying she discovered a way out before they caught up with her.

She pulled up, strangling on a gasp when she whipped around a corner and met a dead end. She blinked at the stark wall in front of her, hands curling and opening at her sides.

"Shit," she muttered, spinning around, her entire body trembling with tension.

She rushed to one door, then another, shaking the latches. All locked. Her nostrils flared, ripe with the scent of her own rising panic.

Hands balling into fists, she braced herself, her chest lifting high with each breath. Several gave chase. She could hear them, their feet slapping hard on the floor. *Feel* them. The fall of their breath, not winded from exertion but the thrill of hunting her.

She shivered at the thought of what they would do to her. Unless she bowed to them as she'd seen Gunter do. Dropped at their feet and promised obedience. *Became one of them.*

Never.

She glanced around again, looking for escape, something she had overlooked. Panic swelled inside her chest. Her nails dug into her palms, cutting the tender skin.

An eerie trickle chased down her spine.

A sense of cool purpose washed through her. *Determination.* Only the feeling was not her own. She was reading it from someone else.

She looked up, and bit back a scream.

12

Her stifled scream twisted to a sob of relief.

Sebastian stared down at her from an open air vent. Sebastian. Alive. The sight of him swinging from the vent in a single move filled her with awe. His muscles rippled as he wrapped one arm around her and plucked her off her feet.

He pulled her up through the duct with him and secured the screen back in place . . . the exact moment footsteps barreled into the hall below and came to an abrupt stop under them.

A voice below snapped something in a guttural tongue she couldn't understand—didn't even recognize as Turkish.

Ruby raised her eyes to Sebastian, parting her lips

to speak. He shook his head at her, the glint of his eyes in the confined, dark space fierce with warning. She realized she could *see* all of him in the pitch black: the gleaming pulse of his muscles ticking beneath grimy, sweat-streaked skin. The way his throat worked with each breath. He now wore pants. Yusuf's. They hung low on his lean hips, drawing attention to his washboard abs. She could see everything perfectly. As if she possessed night vision. Another consequence of her newly altered state.

Biting voices sniped back and forth below. Ruby bit her lip, waiting, flinching when Sebastian closed cold fingers around hers. Still so cold. His hunger came to her then. Frightened at the force of it, she snatched her hand back. At the sound of fading footsteps, she slid away from him over the slick metal.

He jabbed a finger behind her, motioning for her to continue moving. She gave a jerky nod and crawled backward, unable to turn her body until she met an intersection in the ducts. Then Sebastian moved ahead of her, leading the way.

Sounds and shouts drifted on the air. At one point feet raced beneath them, and she knew they were still being hunted. No doubt their smell lingered, easy to detect. Both she and Sebastian were covered in blood. But then blood laced the entire building.

Even the blood from past kills seeped from the floors and walls . . . the very bones of the old structure.

Sebastian finally stopped and opened another screen, working quietly. Sliding the screen free, he dipped his head out and surveyed below before dropping down, silent on the balls of his feet.

She followed, lowering herself into his waiting hands. She glanced around, recognizing the large foyer with its tiled floor and artwork on the walls. Elated to see the door that she had entered through days ago.

He reached it first, closing one hand around the latch, pulling it open the moment a low growl sounded behind them.

A quick glance over her shoulder revealed a man, good-looking in a whipcord-lean marathon cyclist way. His dark blond hair gleamed brightly, alive with lighter, sun-bleached strands, the contrast of sun-kissed hair shocking against his tanned skin.

A light glimmered at the center of his eyes, reminding her of Sebastian. Several others stood behind him, lycans all, with their eerie pewter eyes. Her gaze drifted back to the golden one and his eyes that shone fire. Not a lycan. There was some relief in that. But not much. Because she knew he was dovenatu. With those eyes, he had to be.

"Go." Sebastian shoved her outside, remaining

wedged in the threshold, squaring off against the small throng before them.

He would fight them so she could escape?

She shook her head. She couldn't let him do that for her. Not again. Not when she was a lycan now—with power and strength of her own. She could help him. Help them. They were so close. Why couldn't they run for it together?

"What are you doing?" she hissed, tugging on his arm, feeling again his hunger that felt on the verge of snapping. He couldn't take them all on. Not in his condition. He had to flee.

"Go!" He shook her off. "Get away from here. Run!" His gaze flicked to her then, clung for a moment. "From me."

She sucked in a deep breath, catching his meaning. Feeling it. The cold determination. He would either kill Gunter and save her. Or destroy her. Because as long as her alpha lived, she would be a lycan, a monster. A monster he made it a point to hunt. How could she forget?

With a grunt, she started to turn, ready to flee, only she hesitated a breath when she saw the golden one's face shift, flicker in and out, the features blur as if they were made of nothing more substantial than water . . . the way Sebastian's face had been when he shifted. Into a dovenatu.

Sebastian's voice roared in her head even as she moved. "Run, Ruby—run!"

She plunged into the early evening, nearly blinded from the fading red-gold gleam of light. Leaving death and the cloying smell of blood behind, only one thought burned through her mind: *another dovenatu, another dovenatu.*

How many were there? Sebastian made it sound as if he were an anomaly. He and his brother. But if he wasn't . . . If there were more . . . Not all good ones, like Sebastian—what did that mean for the world?

Shaking her head, she pushed ahead, amazed at the blur of everything around her, at the speed in which she moved.

Feet pounded after her, reminding her that she wasn't the only thing fast as wind. They closed in on her.

She whipped past buildings and yawning doorways with loitering figures. Dark, watchful eyes followed her movement with cautious detachment, ducking back in their dwellings, shoulders hunkering low. Already they knew what she fought to deny. She was something to be feared. Reviled.

She hoped to lose her pursuers in the market, but the bazaar hummed with very little activity. A few vendors hung about, gathering their wares. Even fewer shoppers traveled the warren of streets. Was it some kind of holiday? In the distance, ferry horns mingled with mournful cries calling to prayer. Now, when thousands bowed in the fading dusk, with soulless beasts hunting her, she never felt more alone. Or more abandoned by God.

The quick fall of her feet echoed through the narrow streets. A look over her shoulder revealed three lycans behind her, all male. Their eyes shot silver heat at her, deadly and determined for her blood. They moved with certain purpose, not winded or fatigued. Smiles played on their lips. They were enjoying this. The hunt. They toyed with her, let her run like a mouse ahead of them, fooling her into thinking she had a chance.

Panic fed her heart, made her pump her legs harder. She had the sensation of being a gazelle with hungry lions on her heels in an open space.

She had power, could move fast, but so could they. She needed to think, put an end to this flight of panic and adopt some strategy. Wouldn't Sebastian do that? With a grunt, she shoved thoughts of Sebastian away. She needed to stop thinking of them as connected. Stop thinking about him. Start concentrating on herself.

Feeling exposed in the open, she dove into a side street leading off the square. Brown and tan buildings rose up to stretch against the skyline. A perfect place to get lost.

She dove into a dilapidated tenement, hoping to lead them a merry chase through the halls and rooms of the building, then slip away before they knew she had left.

On the third floor, she ducked inside a room, startling a woman sitting at her sewing machine. Closing the door behind her, she pressed a finger to her lips. Having no idea whether the woman would honor the request, she burst inside a bedroom and flung open the window. Hopping onto the sill, she hovered a moment, her heart in her throat as she wondered just how deeply her powers ran.

Avoiding looking down, she stared at the balcony across from her in the neighboring building, almost on line with the third floor window where she perched. Exhaling, she jumped and sailed through air, wind hissing past.

She caught hold of the balcony with both hands and pulled her body up. Swinging a leg over the railing, she turned to see if her movements were followed. No sight of her pursuers. Shaking with adrenaline, she turned, ready to disappear back into the streets and find her way out of this mad world and catch the first plane home. Back to her life. Her house. Her kitchen with its familiar pots and pans. Adele. And the solitude that she was convinced would never feel lonely or oppressive again.

She found the stairs and descended, plunging back outside. She darted down another street. Certain the fierce pounding of her feet could be heard within miles, she fell into a fast clip. Of course, covered in blood as she was, they could likely sniff out her scent.

The call to prayer ended, and she knew the streets would soon fill with more people again. She needed to change clothes before that happened. Fortunately, her fanny pack still clung to her hips.

Another block and she found a small shop. Ducking inside, she suffered the shop keeper's shrewd stare. He observed her in silence as she picked a woman's caftan from a rack. Hoping to blend in more with the locals, she hurried to the counter, dug out money from the zippered pouch and handed it to the man. She clutched the garment close. As though she could will it on her body and shed her ruined clothes. The shopkeeper pointed to a narrow door shielded with dangling beads. He shot off several words, one of which she understood. "*Tuvalet. Tuvalet.*"

With a grateful nod, she ducked through the beads and found the bathroom, quickly changing into the flowing garment, her fanny pack beneath the copious fabric. Stroking the purple fabric, she inspected herself in the small cracked mirror above the sink, startled at the silver eyes looking back at her, for a moment thinking she had been discovered, that another lycan had hunted her down. Then she realized it was only her reflection, her new eyes, new face. That of an animal.

Vowing to think about that later—to solve that new, not so small glitch in her life after she was safe—she shoved her ruined clothing into a trash bin and hurried from the shop, growing more at ease with every moment. More people merged onto the streets now, and she tried to appear natural as she strolled in—she hoped—the general direction of her hotel. Amid all her running, she had gotten turned around.

"Pardon me? Would you mind helping us?"

Ruby jumped at the soft touch of a hand on her arm before she realized that the voice spoke English. With an American accent. She followed that hand up to the arm of a woman wearing a trendy plum-red trench coat. Her head was bent as she struggled with a city map of Istanbul. Beyond her stood a tall man, very GQ in his black shirt and jeans. He looked slightly bored with his companion's difficulties. He gave Ruby a look of apology, one shoulder shrugging.

The woman muttered over her map. Ruby wanted to hug her in that moment, so relieved to be around someone that reminded her of home. Just looking at the woman made all that she fled seem far away. A distant dream. She felt that much closer to home.

She stepped nearer, ready to confess that she was actually the one in need of help.

Then the woman lifted her face and locked her gaze on Ruby. Her silver gaze. Knowing and calculating. Smug. A predator Ruby knew well. This was no chance meeting. They'd fooled her, drew her in like a net-snared fish.

She slid back a step, colliding into the lycan's companion. His hands closed around her arms. A quick glance behind revealed the familiar pale light dancing at the centers of his eyes. A dovenatu.

She was right back where she started. Only this time, she didn't have Sebastian with her. Even though she knew that was for the best, the thought left her cold and empty. She shivered.

Once again, home seemed very far away.

13

Ruby jerked against the hands wrapped around her, holding her immobile.

"An American. What a coincidence," the lycaness mused, then shrugged. "We were hoping you could take us to your alpha," the woman finished, her voice still oddly kind despite the glittering silver eyes that spelled death.

"Go to hell." Ruby struggled harder against the hands, craning her head to try and glimpse again the threat behind her.

The female shook her head, dark waves of hair tossing as she reached inside her pocket. The hands on Ruby's arms tightened.

A decidedly un-American voice near her ear bit out, "Hurry, Lily. Now."

Ruby glanced over her shoulder: The light that gleamed where his irises should be burned into her. In a surge of strength, she twisted in his arms. Opening her mouth, she started to spit out that she knew what he was, all right . . . she knew that he was worse than a lycan because he had control, a choice, and he chose this. A lycan at his side. Darkness in his heart. He was nothing like Sebastian.

A stabbing pain in her shoulder stopped the words. She gasped. The monster at her back pressed two fingers against the side of her neck and all ability to speak, to utter a sound, vanished.

She slapped a hand over her shoulder, groping wildly until she felt something. Lily's fist—the slim fingers wrapped around a syringe buried in Ruby's shoulder.

She arched, tried to pull the needle free from her body, but Lily beat her to it, tucking it away inside her coat with a covert glance around her. "We're good," she murmured.

A rush of pin-pricks cascaded over Ruby's body. She sagged against her captor, head suddenly spinning. Whatever had been in that needle spread through her. As quickly as wildfire, lethargy sank in.

Total numbing exhaustion. She would have fallen to the ground if not for the dovenatu holding her up.

The lycaness materialized on her other side, taking her arm. Ruby blinked at her face, beautiful but for the silver eyes. The dovenatu gripped her other arm. With Ruby lolling like a rag doll between them, they walked. Her feet didn't work, but it didn't matter. They were strong enough to support her. Her feet skimmed the ground. Anyone who looked at them would probably think she had hit the *raki* too hard.

Ruby looked back and forth between them. Their images grew fuzzy. They carried her toward a parked car. She didn't resist, could not even utter a sound as they secured her in the back seat. Still, she worked her lips, trying to speak, put her vague thoughts into speech, to push the words up past her throat. No use.

The dovenatu climbed behind the wheel.

Then they were moving, the motion of the car rhythmic. She slumped, sliding to her side. The seat beneath her nose smelled of worn leather and sweat. Their voices rolled on the air, but she could not concentrate on their words no matter how she tried. Her thoughts ran a sluggish trail, like a train chugging up a mountain.

Her eyes drifted shut, only one thought able to stick, to penetrate. *Sebastian*. He'd helped her escape, threw himself into danger for her. For nothing.

She prayed that he, at least, had escaped. That at least one of them found freedom. One of them would survive.

Sebastian jumped from building to building, legs launching him far and high. He inhaled the air. The fresh smell of his own blood mingled with the soft aroma of settling night. He bore several wounds. A gouge at his neck. Chest. Arm. He was almost fully regenerated, but blood still soaked him.

His stomach was his first priority. Before he lost it totally—finally—and took down some innocent bystander in a starving fit. He broke into a darkened bakery and gorged himself on breads, sticky baklava and spinach-stuffed pies, and swallowed a gallon of juice from the back refrigerator. And he still hungered, could eat more, but he forced himself to stop. He could eat again later. The clamoring ache had been appeased. For now, he had to find Ruby.

Soon he prowled atop another building. He snatched a man's shirt off a laundry line, studying the streets far below as he pulled it over his head. Ruby was out there somewhere. He felt her. Knew she still lived. He had to reach her. Before any other lycan did . . . or before the dovenatu that he had escaped from at Gunter's nest found him. At least what once was Gunter's nest. Now some other pack had seized it. A pack who had a dovenatu at the helm—a fact that settled like rocks in his gut.

Apparently Sebastian, his brother and Kit weren't the only ones out there. Looking out at the night, he picked up a scent. One he knew all too well. His throat tightened.

"Rafe," he breathed, not really all that surprised his brother was in Istanbul. He would have come, too. The moment he sensed Rafe was in danger. He would have sensed his pain these last weeks. It had been simply too intense for him to disguise.

He soared onto another building, the scent growing closer as he moved, landing like a cat on the balls of his feet from one surface to the next.

His brother was close. He moved toward him, following the thread. In the deepening twilight, he landed on the rooftop of a crowded restaurant. Voices and laughter floated from below, rising on the night with the tempting smells of grilled lamb. He stood, waiting, only a moment before his brother burst through the roof's door.

"Seb," he cried, embracing him. "I knew you were alive."

They had lived apart for so long, Rafe consumed in his role of savior, infiltrated deep in EFLA, the European Federation of Lycan Agents, saving all Marshans marked for death. That was what he did. He helped people, used his skills to save lives, whereas Sebastian simply hunted and destroyed every lycan he came across . . . even the occasional lycan agent if the urge seized him. If he felt justified.

Rafe pulled back to look him over. "God, you're thin."

"A little starvation never killed anyone."

His brother failed to laugh at that. A face identical to his own, only fuller and lacking a beard, stared at him intently, the eyes knowing, traveling down the dark paths that Sebastian had lived in the last months, "Seb . . . you didn't . . ."

"No," he ground out, jaw aching in a tight clench, knowing what his brother was asking. "But it's what they wanted me to do. Bastards." An image of Ruby flashed in his head, bleeding and suffering, enduring her transition in that dank little cell. And all because of him. Because they wished to corrupt him.

And she was still out there. A lycan now. He blinked hard. He had to find her. Before some lycan did. Or that dovenatu he'd narrowly escaped. Or a trigger-happy lycan hunter. His head spun from the possibilities of all that could happen to her. She needed him.

He noticed his brother was not alone. Beyond him stood a petite blond. "Kit, I take it."

With a sharp little twist of her lips, his brother's wife stepped forward and astonished him with a hug. "Thought you two were twins." Pulling back her arm, she scratched warm fingers across his bristly cheek. "Guess we need to work on that."

"You're married to this little thing?" he teased, hiding his unease at suddenly having another relation— a *female* relation. It had only ever been his mother and Rafe.

He felt pity for his mother, compassion for all his mother had endured . . . raped by a lycan . . . then giving birth to him and Rafe. But he suspected she despised them, even if she had raised them and stood by them. Only he knew of the night she had tried to kill them both. He had never shared that information with Rafe. But he knew, and he never forgot.

A tall man with dark blond hair, arms folded across a well-muscled chest, hovered behind his sister-in-law. Kit's brother, he guessed. A lycan hunter who once worked for NODEAL, America's National Organization of Defense against Evolving and Ancient Lycans.

They nodded to one another. In his old life, Gideon March would have killed him without blinking an eye. Would have seen him as just another lycan to be hunted and destroyed. Until he saved a woman from a lycan's curse, and then married her. *The precise thing you must do for Ruby,* a small voice whispered across his head. Minus the marrying part.

"I was starting to worry we wouldn't find you," Rafe said. "We've been here awhile."

"Would take more than a few lycans to kill me."

"Indeed?"

Sebastian's gaze flew to the owner of that voice. His nostrils flared, immediately recognizing what he was even before seeing the pair of pewter eyes. Eyes without the faintest remorse. As chilling as any lycan's.

"Don't tell me. Darius. The lycan with a soul." Doubt rang in his voice; he didn't care. Not after what he'd endured at the hands of Darius's brethren.

"The lycan who *wants* a soul," Kit corrected. And there was a difference. A lycan with a soul was Ruby. An innocent who had not fed, not taken a life. But she would. If he did not find her before moonrise. If he did not protect the world from her . . . *protect her from himself.* Darius did not possess a soul. He had given it up centuries ago. One look at the hard set of his face and Sebastian knew he had fed, killed countless innocents in the course of his life.Not Ruby. He would not let Ruby go down that path.

He swallowed hard against the lump in his throat, telling himself it was nothing more than obligation, his basic sense of rightness that drove him to find her. Nothing more. Not the overriding need to see her again, smell her, feel her, taste her, *have her* . . .

He looked back at his brother. "You have rooms somewhere not far, I hope. Guns, ammo." He didn't doubt his brother's ability to infiltrate any government's rules and regulations. If he hadn't come fully armed, he would have been so upon the hour of arrival in the city.

"Yes. We're at the Four Seasons."

"Good." He strode for the roof's door. "Let's go and get suited." It felt good. Familiar. To be himself again, on a mission, on the hunt.

Rafe's steps fell hard behind him. "Go where?"

"I have to find someone."

"Someone who?" Rafe demanded, his footsteps and that of his companions reverberating throughout the old building's stairwell as they descended to the street.

Sebastian didn't answer at first. The memory of warm, giving skin flooded him.

He should forget her. Logically, he knew it. He had refrained from killing her. No small feat. He hadn't been the one, after all, to drag her into Gunter's nest. She'd done that all on her own. The mess she was in was her own. He could call it quits. He could. He should.

Ruby's face drifted through his mind, her eyes—

even silver, the warm brown long gone—gleamed at him with knowing, a deep awareness of him. She could see him, the core of him, read him. No woman had before.

Shaking his head, he cursed. He would never forget her. An empath. A person who knew him no matter what barriers he tossed up. She was both compelling and frightening. *And she needs you.*

"I'm going to catch a lycan." The easiest explanation. Even if they did not ring quite true. She was more than a lycan. So much more.

"Bro, we need to care for you first, put some meat back on you, and then we'll talk and plan a way to take out the pack who did this to you."

He didn't have time to wait and lick his wounds. Ruby didn't have that much time. He needed to find her. Then he would go back for her alpha.

Then she would be free.

And so would he.

14

Ruby woke on a comfortable bed, cheerful rays of light spilling through partially-slitted shutters. Gone was her caftan. A simple white tee hugged her torso. Soft velour jogging pants encased her legs. And her body was clean. Her fingers brushed her head, trailed through clean strands of hair.

Despite her state of comfort, an awful taste filled her mouth at the thought of someone undressing her. *Bathing her.* Either the female, Lily, or the dove-natu, it didn't matter. She felt violated. A hot wash of anger shuddered through her.

She sprang to life, vaulting from the bed, not pausing to acclimate to her new surroundings. She didn't need to. She took it all in at a glance. The sparsely furnished yet well-appointed room, the open bedroom door. *Open?*

On her feet, she stopped before the open door. Her captors felt comfortable enough with their prowess that they did not bother to lock her in?

She resisted running through the door, convinced more stealth was required. Turning, she raised the shutters from the window, hoping to find a way out. She growled at the bars lining the window. No escape that way.

"You're awake."

Ruby spun around, facing the female from yesterday. At least she supposed it was yesterday. Who knew how long they drugged her?

"Good afternoon. Have a good rest?"

Ruby sidled along the wall, palms skimming the cool wallpaper, watching Lily carefully. So far she had met with only brutality at the hands of lycans. "Where am I?"

"My husband and I have rented this house while we attend to our business in Istanbul."

Business. She made it sound so professional. Wasn't their business killing and dealing savagery on the world? And who was her husband? That dovenatu? How could *they* be together? Sebastian made it seem such an impossibility. There were lycans. And there were dovenatus, and never the two mixed. Except with these two. Oh, and the golden dovenatu she had seen back at Gunter's nest. He'd been in league with lycans. Apparently the rules were changing. At least as Sebastian knew them.

"And what does your business have to do with me?"

"Well, you're a lycan." She gestured at Ruby, light glinting off the very large diamond wedding ring on her hand.

Angling her head, she studied Ruby. "You're young. And I don't just mean in human years. Newly turned, I'm guessing."

"How can you tell?"

The dovenatu emerged in the doorway then. His large frame dominated the space and Ruby shrank even deeper against the wall.

His wife moved closer to his side, as if linked by a magnetic force. Her husband wrapped an arm around her waist. Ruby stared at the pair. Something was wrong. Well, maybe not wrong, but just . . . *off*. They seemed genuinely besotted with each other. In love. And love was not something she had witnessed—*or felt*—among the lycans of Gunter's pack. According to Sebastian, after a lycan fed, all humanity was lost. Hope stirred in her heart. Maybe there was a way to live with this curse and keep her humanity.

"When were you turned?" Lily asked.

"What day is it?"

The female blinked. "You haven't fed yet, then?"

"No." Ruby stared back and forth between them. "Why should that matter to you?"

"Of course it matters to us. If you haven't fed, then you're . . . you're—" She looked to her husband before turning back to Ruby with unmistakably kind eyes and announcing with great emphasis, "I've never fed either."

Hope swelled over. She took a jerky step away from the wall. "You haven't? Why? How?"

"Because I don't want to," she answered simply, as if there were a choice in the matter. As if stopping herself from shifting and killing every moonrise posed no difficulty. As if sheer will alone could prevent that from happening.

"Every moonrise, I sedate my wife," the dovenatu answered, apparently reading her mind.

She stared at the arm he wrapped so securely around her waist and felt a flash of envy that Lily had such love and devotion from another soul that she could rely on him to see her through every moonrise. She felt the lack in her own life all the more keenly. She didn't have anyone. Perhaps Adele could be counted upon, but Ruby hated to put her at risk. And how could she rely on Adele forever? Adele was mortal . . . would age and die. Then who would safeguard mankind from her? Unbidden, an image of

Sebastian rose in her mind. She shook her head. He was gone. She would never see him again.

"Propofol," Lily volunteered.

"Propofol?"

"It's a sedative. Takes effect almost immediately."

Her knees went weak. So there was a way. She didn't have to live the life of a ravaging beast, cursed, damned, lacking a soul. She didn't need to hope Sebastian would help her find Gunter and put an end to him . . . an end to her curse.

There was a way. *I can go home. I can take back my life.* She must have whispered the words aloud.

Lily smiled. "Well, maybe. But you could help us first before you do."

"How can I help you?" And did she want to? She was over the whole putting herself in jeopardy thing. Maybe that made her selfish, but she didn't care. She had tried to help Amy and Emily, and look where it got her. Sex for the first time with someone who wasn't even human. A scratch that turned her into a lycan. Oh, and gutted from stomach to chest. She was tired. Tired of hurting. Tired of feeling the wretched, black emotions of the monsters around her. She was through, finished. She wanted to go home and lick her wounds.

So she would be this . . . creature. She could handle it. She was used to being different. A freak.

"We don't mean you any harm," the dovenatu murmured.

She focused on him, but she could not pick up any ill feelings, none of the darkness, no beast prowling beneath the surface. Most of his emotions centered on his wife . . . and all those sentiments were tender. Warm.

"We promise to help you. Get you safely wherever you want to go after you do us this favor." *Favor*. She made it sound minor. Small. "Come on." Lily stepped aside, motioning her through the door. "You must be famished. We have brunch laid out. We can eat while we talk.

Her stomach rumbled. "I would like that." She took a deep breath, feeling safe for the first time in days. Safe. And free. Free of that damned cell and those lycans. She could help them. A small thing to do for their help. After she helped them with whatever they needed, she'd be on a plane home.

Minutes later, sitting outside at a wrought-iron table overlooking a heavenly rose garden, taking her first bite of jam-slathered toast and imagining herself back home, she learned what they wanted from her.

"We want you to lead us to the lycans who infected you."

The toast turned to dust on her tongue.

*   *   *

Ivo lounged in the great bed that had once belonged to the alpha of the pack he had just deposed. He listened as Jonah gave an accounting of the day's events. A total of eleven lycans dead: eight of Gunter's pack, three of Ivo's force. Not bad. Not that he cared about the loss of his three, anyway. Lycans were expendable, mere soldiers to him. To be used for his purpose. And his purpose was simple. Amass an army great enough to take on the world, to wipe out EFLA, NODEAL and all humans who dared resist.

"Twenty-one recruited, including Gunter. I don't expect any resistance. I've sent Gunter to the smaller lycan nests outside the city to apprise them that he's been routed and you've taken charge. He should be back in the morning with the necessary tribute from each pack. Not bad work for an afternoon," Jonah reported, his blue gaze flat, his voice its usual clipped monotone.

Ivo studied him, roving small circles with his fingers on his mate's tender flesh. He wished he could read him better. After thirty years, he thought he would have figured the young hybrid out. He'd found him starving in a London slum and instantly known what he was. Taking him under his wing, he trained the dovenatu to be his second-in-command, pleased he'd found another dovenatu to one day breed with his daughters and help toward his goal of creating a master race.

Jonah stared at him, cocking an eyebrow. "Aren't you pleased?"

"Very much," he murmured. "The pack reputed to be the toughest in Istanbul has fallen into my lap with relative ease." There had been far harder conquests. Barcelona had nearly defeated him. He'd wiped that entire pack out for refusing to bend to his authority.

His hand drifted to Danae's belly, the slight bulge there deeply satisfying. Their fifth child. He hoped for another son. Three daughters were well and good, but with Jonah the only male dovenatu around with whom he might breed them, they weren't entirely useful. Too bad his cousin Luc had disappeared years ago, stricken with an overly active conscience. Ivo would have forgotten about the close familiar relation and bred his daughters with his first cousin so that he might create the dynasty of which he dreamed. For now, Jonah would have to be enough.

"You mentioned two escaped?"

"They were prisoners." Jonah shrugged one broad shoulder. He was strong, well-trained from years of fighting and subduing lycans. "I questioned Gunter and learned something you may find interesting, though."

"And that is?"

"One of them was a dovenatu."

Ivo sat up in bed, the silk sheet sliding to his hips. "One of them? The male or female?" His blood burned at the thought of a female dovenatu, one whom he might use to further strengthen and multiple his progeny on the earth. He loved Danae. But love had nothing to do with fidelity. If other female dovenatus existed, he would gladly use them for his purposes.

"The male. The female was a lycan, newly turned."

"Oh." He sat back, only slightly disappointed. A male could serve him just as well, he supposed. As Jonah served him. "Find him. Bring him back at once. Alive. He's no use to me dead. Take a few dogs with you to be of assistance. And don't cause him too much harm bringing him to heel either. Explain our purpose. You might find him obliging." A male dovenatu. He nodded, a smile curving his lips. He would be quite useful. Now he would own two studs for his daughters.

"Of course." Jonah turned.

"And Jonah."

His second-in-command stopped and faced him again, those eyes cool and unreadable as ever. "Yes?"

"When you return, we'll discuss you taking Sorcha."

A faint flicker of emotion passed over his face, and

even then Ivo could not tell exactly what Jonah felt at his declaration.

He continued, "No more talk of her youth. Fifteen is more than ready." At Jonah's stoic expression, he added. "Otherwise, I'm sure this other dovenatu will make a fine stud and have her breeding within the year."

Jonah nodded curtly. "Very well."

Ivo slid his hand back along his wife's thigh. "Now leave us."

The door shut, the sound resounding in the cavernous room. Facing his mate, he shook his head. "I just don't know about that boy."

"Such a prig. Reminds me of your cousin Luc at times. He has that scared look about him."

Ivo shrugged, not too bothered about that. "He's my second-in-command. Wouldn't want him *too* brave and bold. He might think to oppose me."

He smiled then, thinking of his cousin, likely cowering and living the life of a hermit monk somewhere . . . too frightened of himself—of Ivo—of the dark powers that simmered inside them. Luc had not even tried to oppose him. Not even when he claimed Danae. He just ran. "You once liked Luc. You even preferred him to me for a time."

"Never," she purred, wrapping a satiny thigh around his waist. "You're the one I was always after.

The big fish. Luc was weak, not even close to the man you are."

"Not a man, my dear. *A god.*"

Danae stripped her nightgown over her head then and straddled him. His eyes feasted on her as she came down on him. He caressed the large breasts swaying above the belly that carried his seed, one of many offspring that he would breed to serve at his side as he reigned supreme over the world.

Dovenatus. The perfect race. All the strength and prowess of lycans. The ability to shift at will, to *think.* They killed when they willed it. The moon did not rule them. Nothing did.

Soon his sixth child would be born. Soon his daughters would breed. And once EFLA was at his mercy, he would find the location of every Marshan female, drag the information from the EFLA archivists through whatever means necessary and release his lycan soldiers on them. He would have his population of dovenatus. A new world was on the rise.

When he met this other dovenatu, he intended to teach him that particular lesson first thing.

Sorcha whirled around at her younger sisters who crept up behind her with all the stealth of a herd of horses. "Go back to your rooms!"

"You're supposed to be in bed." Rochel, only eighteen months her junior but already bigger in the chest, taunted. "What are you doing? Following Jonah around like a little puppy again? Must sting to know he doesn't want you . . . no matter how many times Father offers you to him. Face it. You're too ugly. Too fat—"

"Shut up, brat," Sorcha hissed, knotting a fist at her side and taking a threatening step in Rochel's direction.

The girl flung her dark hair over one shoulder. "He's probably waiting for me." She puffed out her melon-sized breasts against her nightgown. "He's probably trying to think of a way to not hurt your feelings by taking me to mate. I've seen the way he looks at me." She shivered with delight. "It's like he's picturing me naked!"

"Shut up," she hissed again, wondering how wrong it was to hate your own sister. Or, for that matter, your own father. She grimaced at the thought of him. She had just overheard what he said to Jonah and her fury couldn't burn hotter.

If Jonah didn't want her, Father would give her to some stranger? Her stomach knotted and she feared she would lose her dinner. She couldn't let him do that. Couldn't let him use her as some sort of broodmare in his mad game to dominate the world.

If Jonah didn't want her, she would run away. Some place far, where her father could never find her. She was smart, always with her nose in a book. She spoke five languages—one of the benefits of always moving, never settling anywhere, never having roots, a home. Jonah was the only boy—*man*—to ever spike her interest. He did things to her heart no other man could do.

If he didn't want her, she would have no one.

"Sorcha."

She whirled around at the voice. A voice she knew instantly.

"What are you doing out here?" He looked over her shoulder at her two simpering sisters. Both of them, age ten and fourteen, batted their lashes. It was as though they had been born with active libidos. And she supposed that was the nature of what they were: dovenatus raised at the foot of a man who taught them that their greatest worth would be that of breeding heirs to their race.

"Get to bed," he ordered, his voice biting, leaving no room for argument.

Her sisters scurried off at his command. Sorcha faced Jonah. He stared at her for a moment, and she felt her face heat as she recalled the conversation she had overheard.

"Are your rooms satisfactory?"

"It doesn't matter. In a month, we'll be somewhere else, another city, another nest of lycans for my father to add to his collection. The madness will never stop."

His gaze fixed on her, ever unreadable. "You shouldn't speak that way—"

"Why?"

"Your father wouldn't like it and I would hate to see you punished."

A lump filled her throat. Only he gave a damn. Only ever him.

"You care so much about what he thinks?" She cocked her head to the side. "Then why don't you do what he asks of you?" She couldn't have been more direct.

The light at the center of his blue eyes ignited and she knew he understood her meaning. He inhaled deeply. "Sorcha . . ."

It was the tired way he said her name that did it, convinced her he would never love her. No matter that her father commanded they mate, no matter that they were two of a rare species, ideally suited for each other. No matter how much she cared for him. She was nothing more than the doting puppy her sisters accused her of being. Rochel was probably right. She repulsed him. He thought her too ugly. Too fat.

She held up a hand, stopping him from saying any

more, stopping him from delivering her more humiliation. "I understand. Say no more."

With pity in his gaze, he watched her. Unable to stand it, Sorcha turned, walking quickly, just shy of a run. There was nothing left to keep her here anymore. Hope for a future with Jonah fell dead in her chest.

He would continue to serve her father, and maybe someday he would take one of her sisters to mate. She would never know. Because she wouldn't be here.

Soon, she vowed, she would forget his face. Eventually, his name.

And one day she would not even remember this killing pain in her heart.

15

Dressed, fed again, Sebastian strode through the bazaar near Gunter's nest with swift purpose, feeling almost himself again. Almost. All expect the tightness seizing his throat when he thought about Ruby. Out there alone. He detected traces of her, hints, but nothing substantial lingered. She was long gone, beyond tracking. It was as if she had disappeared like smoke from the streets. Plucked off the ground and whisked away on the wind.

Since they'd mated, he was tuned in to her. He knew the earthy scent of her skin, the aroma of her hair. Wind that passed over her tasted different on his lips, felt different against his face. Lifting his chin, he breathed, drawing air deeply into his chest, probing.

There was a bite in the air. It nipped at his newly shaved cheeks. Lowering his chin, he settled his gaze before him, eyes straight ahead as he walked.

He could pick up nothing.

"So," Kit murmured, keeping pace beside him. "Is this lycan pretty?"

Sebastian glared at his sister-in-law. In the last day, he had learned how strong-willed she could be. And nosy. There was no leaving her behind at the hotel. In fact, they *all* insisted on joining him in his search.

This close to the pack's nest, he knew he risked discovery. Darius, it seemed, knew this, too. Several times, the lycan would pause and lift his face to the air. Then his gaze would find Sebastian's, lock in silent message. *They risked much.* And yet Darius never objected as they circled dangerously close to the pack's nest again and again. He supposed a thousand-year-old lycan was accustomed to risking death.

"What are we doing hunting this one lycan?" Gideon demanded of Rafe. "We found your brother—not that it appeared we needed to. He's safe now—"

"Then go home, March," Sebastian snapped, stopping at a sudden familiar scent. Just the barest trickle, but he marked it. *Ruby.*

He moved past vendors' stalls, slapping at a colorful array of scarves that blew in his path.

"Sebastian! Wait up," Rafe called but he was gone, on the scent.

Her smell grew stronger and his gut cramped as he realized he was headed directly for the nest. Had she been recaptured then? His pulse hammered in his ears as he flew through the narrow alley, stopping before bursting into the courtyard that faced the warehouse of horrors he and Ruby had survived together.

"What are we doing here?" Rafe stopped beside him.

Sebastian held up a hand, listening, *feeling*. He sensed her close, but she wasn't inside the warehouse. No, she was . . .

His gaze drifted up to the tenement at his right. Several shadowed and curtained windows stared down at him. Watching eyes.

He turned and ran for the front door. The others pounded behind him. He blew up three flights of stairs before stopping. A baby cried from a room somewhere at the end of the floor. He eased his foot off the top step and started down the dingy hall, each step he took slow, measured and assessing, before halting at the door numbered 417.

He resisted the instinct to burst inside the room. His skin tightened, pulled with familiar, snapping tension. Instead, he closed his hand around the latch, wondering why she would be this close to the nest.

Wouldn't she have wanted to get as far as possible from the pack? What he knew of her led him to think so, but then what did he really know of the woman he had ravished within the first twenty-four hours of meeting? Other than that she had every reason to hate him. Fear him. He winced at the reminder, then shoved the memories away. Especially the ones that made his blood burn—the silken heat of her surrounding him, taking him deep inside her body. Steeling himself, he pushed open the door.

His eyes locked on a male, not a lycan . . . but not human either. The light gleaming at the centers of his eyes marked him a dovenatu. Damn, another one. That brought their total count in this city to who knew what. Clearly, EFLA's and NODEAL's attempts to control the breeding of dovenatus had failed, and their extermination of all Marshan descendants was all the more pointless. Sebastian, Rafe and Kit weren't the only hybrids. This city was overrun with them.

His brother and the others crowded close behind him, their breaths falling hard and heavy. The bastard was so big, easily pushing six and a half feet. He overpowered the room with his proportions. Sebastian took a moment to locate Ruby.

Sebastian felt her—the very pulse of her life's blood reached out to him across the squalid little room—before he located her. She stepped around the dovenatu. Her fingers circled his muscled forearm, and the action sent the blood pumping hard and fierce through him.

"Sebastian!" Her gaze scanned his face, eyes widening as she took her first good look. She hadn't seen him like this before. Clean. Shaved. Civilized. In truth, this was the first time she had ever been granted the full view of his face. Stupidly, foolishly, he felt a surge of self-consciousness, hoping she liked what she saw. That the sight of him—the man who had ravaged her on the floor of a cold, dirty room and claimed her virginity—did not disappoint her.

Tension thickened the air.

"Yeah," he bit out, his voice tight with anger. "I'm alive." She looked good. Skin a healthy glow. Dark hair falling past her shoulder in glossy waves. "In case you were concerned." His gaze flicked back to her hand on the stranger, and he inwardly cursed himself for sounding like a petulant child, jealous and sniping.

Frowning, Ruby tried to step forward then, but the dark-haired hybrid wouldn't let her. He stopped her, one hand clamping down on her arm.

Red filled Sebastian's vision, and he sprang into action, unmoved by the cries from those behind him. He crashed into the other hybrid, sending them to the ground in a fierce collision. Bone met bone as he struck the bastard. The floor shuddered beneath their thrashing weight and from the ferocity of their blows. His head snapped back from a punch that would have knocked a normal man's head from his shoulders.

He heard Ruby scream, and his heart squeezed a little. Did she scream for him? Because she gave a damn? Or because she wanted him to leave off killing her new *friend*?

His brother and Kit fell on him, tugged him back, using every bit of their considerable strength. Darius squared off before the hybrid, stopping him from charging.

Ruby positioned herself in front of Sebastian, hands on her hips, pewter eyes aglow. "What are you doing?" Looking back over her shoulder at the imposing wall Darius made in front of her friend, she abandoned him in a flash.

"Leave him alone!" she cried.

Air sawed from his lungs, frothing at his lips. He steeled himself, trying to regain his composure, to not sink into the dark and let the beast overrun him because Ruby appeared to care for another over him.

"I thought I was saving your ass," he snarled to her earlier demand, as if she still gave a damn and waited for his answer. He eyed her proximity to the dovenatu, the way she insinuated herself between Darius and him. Almost as though she thought she needed to protect the hybrid from *them*. "Guess I was wrong. It appears you don't need saving."

"You *are* wrong," she agreed with force. "I don't."

Only what he heard was: *I don't need you.*

It stung. More than it should. He quickly squashed the feeling. The last thing he wanted was for her to use her gift and sense his feelings, to think he was hurt or rejected. He didn't want her in his head. Especially not right now when jealousy ripped through him at her closeness to some stranger.

"My mistake, then." He shrugged out of his brother's and Kit's hold. "Let's go." Vowing inwardly to leave her and forget her, he didn't stop when he heard her call his name. She could have her damned hybrid. She could shift at the next moonrise and kill, feed, lose her soul . . .

He did stop, however, when a female lycan arrived breathlessly in the door, her dark hair wild and wind-tossed around her shoulders, as if she had run a great distance at the speed only one of their kind could achieve.

"Luc," she rasped, her gaze landing on the hybrid before skimming each of them, assessing them for threat. Her throat worked, her pewter gaze wild. "Are you okay?"

"Everyone, just stop! Don't move!" Ruby sliced

a hand through the air. "We're all on the same side here." She flicked Darius—dark, imposing Darius—a nervous glance. "I think."

"He's all right," Sebastian ground out, to which Ruby release a shaky little breath of relief.

"Isn't all this . . . interesting." Darius looked between Ruby and the new female with burning intensity, his interest in the pair palpable. They *were* him, after all. Full-blooded lycans driven by hunger—moon hunger, blood hunger—and ruled by the impulses of their libido. Either one would be a perfect mate for him . . . at least that must be what his instinct was screaming.

Luc strode past Darius and took hold of the other female's hand in a possessive display. The brunette pressed close to his side. Luc sent Ruby a pointed look. "Ruby, who are these . . . people?"

She motioned to him. "Sebastian is the dovenatu I told you about."

Sebastian bristled at their familiarity, but stood his ground.

Luc looked hard at him. "And these are your friends, I gather?"

"That's right." He guessed it was the easiest explanation, although he didn't know whether he would call Gideon and Darius friends. Gideon—he supposed he was family now. But Darius? He didn't trust the guy. Doubtful he ever could trust a lycan—

He stopped hard at the thought, thinking of Ruby. His gaze snapped back to her. Dressed in fresh clothes. Body washed and clean hair shining darkly. She had been covered in blood and filth most of their time together. He drank this sight of her hungrily. Even with her silver death gaze, she was better, sweeter on the eyes than he remembered.

"If we're all on the same side, maybe you could help us, then," the female lycan suggested.

"Lily," Luc murmured, his gaze sliding over each of them warily. "We know nothing of them."

"Well, they aren't over there, are they? With *them*? That has to mean something." She motioned in the general direction of the warehouse, then turned her gaze on Sebastian. "Why are you here?" He thought he read hope in her expression. A motherly type of encouragment. His imagination, of course.

"I came for Ruby."

"Oh. And why is that?" Luc pushed out his chest and crossed his arms.

Lily elbowed him in the side and addressed Sebastian. "Of course you came for her. Ruby told us all about your imprisonment together." The lycaness smiled widely, a dose of civility that ran opposite to the moment. "You saved her life."

Sebastian's gaze locked on Ruby. Color flooded

her cheeks, and he knew she was thinking about their imprisonment together. Specifically the portion of it spent having hot, wild sex with him. Had she told them about that?

"Look," Luc announced. "We're here for one reason only, and that's to track down and destroy the family of dovenatus in that building." He nodded to Ruby. "We found Ruby and she helped us pinpoint Ivo's location."

"Dovenatus?" Kit broke in. "How many are we talking about?" Like Sebastian, she clearly grappled with the information that more of their kind existed.

"I suspect there are more of us than we realize," Luc answered grimly. "Ivo's a madman, determined to promote our species by enslaving lycans, then using them to . . . come out."

"Come out?" Sebastian asked.

"Yeah," Lily announced, with obvious disgust. "With an army of lycans at his disposal, he intends to proclaim himself to the world and subjugate man."

"And if we don't want to be enslaved?" Rafe asked, lines tightening around his mouth.

"Then he kills you. Or sics his lycan soldiers on you." Luc shrugged. "He's got an army of them pledged in service to him."

"How can that be?" Kit questioned, "Don't lycans outnumber him?"

"Lycans are fiercely pack-loyal. They serve one alpha and war against all other packs. Their inability to unite is their greatest weakness. Ivo's army grows with every pack taken, he becomes their alpha . . ." Luc stopped, shaking his head. "I can't imagine how many packs he's taken since he started on this mad scheme. It might be too late. He should have been stopped long ago."

"You sound like you know this Ivo well."

"I do." Luc glanced at his wife. "He's my cousin. We grew up together. Perhaps we're even half brothers." He shrugged. "I'll never know. Our mothers were sisters, Marshan descendants both raped by lycans, together. On the same day."

"And you're here to destroy him. Your own relative." Kit snorted, crossing her arms and spreading her booted legs. "You sure about that? How do we know you won't chicken out? That when you come face to face you won't give him a great big hug?"

Rafe had told Sebastian she was a lycan hunter—excepting Darius—but he had never really appreciated that until now. Until he saw this hardness in her. This edge.

"It's the only way to stop him. To make this world safer." He shot Lily a tender glance. "For my family."

Sebastian tore his gaze from Ruby, stopping any tender feelings from rising up in him at the display of affection between a lycan and a dovenatu. "And how were you thinking about doing this?"

Luc and Lily exchanged looks. She took his hand in hers. "He never stays in one nest long after he conquers it. He's almost impossible to track that way, and it's nearly impossible to get close to him—"

"What is your plan?" Sebastian bit out, his patience at an end.

"We're going after them. Tonight," Lily explained. "Before they move."

At Sebastian's arched brow, Luc answered. "We're going to blow up the warehouse."

Air hissed out between his teeth. While silver was the most common method used to kill a lycan, being blown into a million fragments was another. Sometimes EFLA and NODEAL employed that measure when they tracked down a nest.

From Ruby's wide eyes, the plan was news to her.

"Any additional help would be appreciated." Luc's tone turned matter-of-fact. He motioned to several crates sitting on one side of the room. "We need to make sure all the charges are clear and unobstructed around the perimeter. And explosives positioned on every floor of the building. No one can survive. We're looking for total incineration."

"We have to go back in there?" Ruby's face paled, and Sebastian felt a surge of protectiveness.

"Ruby's been through enough," he spoke up. "I'm taking her to the hotel."

She gave a small jerk, clearly startled at his words. "I don't need a babysitter, thank you. I'm a big girl."

"You're coming with me."

Their gazes clung. The air crackled between them. His hands flexed at his sides. He'd carry her if he had to. She wasn't putting herself at risk anymore.

"Wait." She blinked, shaking her head, color heightening her cheeks as she came to a sudden realization. "If Gunter's in there during the explosion—"

"Your curse will be broken," Lily finished, reaching over to give her hand a small squeeze, smiling kindly.

Ruby returned her smile. A shaky sigh spilled from her lips, and she closed her eyes in a long relieved blink.

"I'll stay and assist however I can," Darius volunteered.

Luc nodded, eyeing Darius warily, as if he was unsure whether he wanted his help.

"What the hell?" Gideon shrugged. "Came all this way. Suppose I will, too."

"Oh, no, you don't." Kit shook her head fiercely. "Claire will have my head if anything happens to you. You have a baby at home waiting for Daddy. Rafe and I will help. Not you." Rafe nodded in agreement.

Gideon scowled. "Claire knew I was taking a risk coming here. I'm in."

Shaking his head, Sebastian stepped forward and closed a hand around Ruby's arm, the warmth of her flesh instantly familiar and sweet. "Let's go."

He'd spent enough time in that warehouse. As had Ruby. He'd fantasized about revenge for weeks, but now he cared more about keeping Ruby safe. He owed her that.

He wasn't inclined to risk her another moment to the bastards prowling that warehouse. He would let the others rig the explosives. They'd do the job right. Kill Gunter.

Right now Ruby needed him. He wasn't leaving her until this was over.

He faced his brother. "See you back at the hotel. Be safe."

With one hand wrapped around Ruby's, he hurried them from the building to wait out the outcome across town.

16

"Why did you come back for me?" She spoke quietly where she sat on the backseat of the cab, looking out the window rather than at him. Anywhere but him. She gnawed the edge of her thumbnail. A bad habit she thought she'd outgrown long ago.

With his face shaved, body clean, dressed in a simple black t-shirt and jeans, he was overwhelming to her senses. Her gaze skittered to him. Outside the cell, he seemed even larger, his shirt stretched taut over his defined chest. And who knew *that* face hid beneath all that hair? Her heart beat an erratic rhythm in her too-tight chest. Gorgeous in a very David Beckham way. The square jaw, the chiseled lips that looked made for kissing.

She felt his answer before he even spoke, felt it rise up inside him and reach out to her. *Bewilderment. Anger.* The anger was not with her, but at himself. This she knew.

She lowered her hand from her lips. Her fingers floated above the seat for a moment, the barest tremble over his. The urge to wrap her fingers over his hand seized her. *He came for me.* Her throat grew tight. That was more than anyone else in her life would do. He cared enough to track her down, find her and keep her from returning to that nest again. Sitting beside him, so close she could smell the light scent of shampoo, something inside her loosened, unfurled inside her chest. Then she regained her senses and snatched her hand away to fist it in her lap.

"I don't know." He scratched his fingers through his short-cropped hair. "We seemed connected in all this. I couldn't be done with any of it until I knew you were safe. Free."

"Well." She fingered the edge of the seat. "Now I am. So you're done." She moistened her lips, her mouth suddenly dry at speaking words she didn't want to be true.

"Almost."

She sent him a sideways look on the seat, gazing at the hard line of his jaw. A muscle flexed in his taut cheek and her insides quivered—all the way deep, to the core of her. Where she remembered him. Where the hard burn of him had filled her. Thrilling. Terrifying. Wrong. *Right*.

"What do you mean, almost?"

"When they set off that bomb and Gunter's dead, then it will be truly over."

Her nails dug into the upholstery. "That shouldn't be too long."

Tension swam between them. Except for the driver, they were alone again. Every fiber of her being radiated with awareness of him, his arm so close it nearly brushed her. His tightly-muscled body hummed with vitality beside her. Strength. Power. Her palms itched.

When they finally arrived at the hotel, she slid out eagerly from the cab. Side by side, they entered the luxurious hotel. At the front desk, Sebastian acquired a room for her on the same floor as his. "Your room is next to mine," he murmured as the elevator ascended. "Just knock if you need anything."

She moistened her lips. "Thank you." He unlocked her door and handed her the key. Their fingers brushed and air hissed from between her teeth at the contact. Breathless, she heard herself saying, "I don't think I can be by myself. In this city. Not yet."

He stared at her for several moments. The feral chill in that dark gaze made her want to shiver, flinch, look away. She held her ground, releasing her breath when he broke eye contact and walked past her into her room.

Now they were truly alone again. Like before. No driver to bear silent witness. In a clean room. With a large, tempting bed.

She unhooked her money belt and dropped it on a table. Moving to the small bar, she asked, "Drink?"

"No, thank you."

She poured herself a glass of something golden-brown. She couldn't make out the label, but it burned going down. She filled it a second time, gasping when his large hand covered hers. "Don't."

"What?"

"You don't have to drink yourself to oblivion. It's almost over. Tomorrow you can go home and put it all behind you."

"Really?" Her head snapped back, the drink spreading like fire through her belly. Her eyes collided with his. "And what about you? Will I forget you?"

He flinched. A muscle jumped wildly in his jaw.

She reached for the glass again, her voice hard, bitter over the heaviness in her chest, the tight ache surrounding her heart. "Because that might be hard to do."

"What do you want me to do about that now, Ruby? I can't take it back. Not any of it."

"Do you even care? Are you even sorry?" She

heard the sharpness of her voice, felt the rise of heat in her face and knew that she was dangerously close to snapping.

"Sorry? Sorry for being something that had to either fuck you or devour you." He dragged a hand through his hair and flung himself away from her; stood before the window. He faced the city skyline. The night burned with a thousand lights.

She drew a shuddering breath.

His voice continued in a low, dark rush, "Hell, yes. I'm sorry. Sorry for what I am." His dark eyes glittered, sucking her in, spiking heat inside her. "Sorry that when you look at me all you will ever remember is the suffering we shared together."

She shook her head. His regret, the hurt he felt, reached inside her, twisting her stomach.

Her mother warned her of this. *You cannot take others' hurt inside you, Ruby. You can't cure them of it, so don't make it your own. Throw up your walls, do whatever you can to protect yourself.*

Easier said than done. Especially where he was concerned. All she ever did around him was *feel*. He was impossible to block. And she had learned to block over the years, as her mother advised. To some degree. Otherwise, she couldn't function. But with him, Sebastian . . . Her heart wouldn't close itself. So she felt his regret, and wondered why she didn't feel the same. Why did she only want him to take her in his arms?

"Don't." She moved to his side and touched his shoulder. "Don't hate what you can't help being."

Her words brought her up hard. Had she not done that very thing for most of her life? Didn't Adele nag her to embrace her gift? Although she doubted she could ever open up shop declaring herself clairvoyant and charge thirty dollars an hour, she could learn to better accept herself.

He looked down at her, his gaze pulling her in. "I guess you know something about that."

She laughed nervously. How could she forget? He knew her secret. "Not many know that about me." She wished he didn't. Wished she could take back the confession. She would give anything for him to not look at her as her own family had . . . a freak of nature.

His gaze drilled into her and she began to feel something else beneath the tension of the moment. His skin beneath her hand began to spark and tingle, warm. "You're not cold anymore," she murmured, moistening her lips. "Before, when we were locked up, you were so cold."

"I've eaten." His lips twisted. A full mouth, she now appreciated, teeth a blinding flash of white. "I'm no longer a walking corpse."

He lifted a hand and brushed the hair back off her shoulder. She jumped at the contact. His thumb grazed her cheek and he tilted her face up to his.

Step back. Move away, Ruby.

Instead, she gazed up at him, his face limned in red from the city lights outside their window. He looked menacing, but she didn't care. Danger had become as natural to her as the air she breathed, and she discovered she craved this particular brand of danger. *She craved him.*

Tonight her curse would end, and she would go back to Beau Rivage. She could forget that she had ever been some terrible creature of myth. She could forget him and pretend that she had not given herself to him on the floor of a dirty cell, like a pair of wild animals.

"You know what I'm feeling," he murmured, his eyes penetrating. "So why are you still standing here? Letting me touch you like this?"

She swallowed. She did know. And the desire swelling through him, the hot sexual need, should have her demanding that he leave.

Except she felt it, too. Deep inside her. It drove her to the edge. Drove her to forget everything except the hot pulse of lust.

"I've always been safe. Done what I should." Except for this trip. This trip had been her first foray into the unknown. And after everything that had happened, she should have learned her lesson about taking risks, venturing into the unknown. But she still stood here. Welcoming danger head-on—*him*. "Tomorrow I'll be safe again." Human. On a plane to the States.

She licked her lips. The memory of his hands on her hips, warm and firm, anchoring her for his every penetrating thrust, flashed through her head. Her hips tingled, as if she could feel his hands on her again, now, holding her for his driving pleasure.

Her voice slipped past her lips. "I want you. Without the fear." No rushed, desperate coupling. She wanted it to be right this time.

"Ruby." The callused pads of his hand chafed her cheek.

She thought of those few dates she had risked over the years . . . the men that had repelled her with their lukewarm emotions, their lack of interest reaching her before their drinks even arrived. Or those whose obnoxious and lewd thoughts made her skin crawl.

"You don't want me. This is the lycan talking. Your libido is overactive now. It's one of the many changes—"

"No." She shook her head. He was the first person she ever felt this way with—it was him. "It's not that. It's me. You."

"You only think—"

She cut him off again. "I want it to be right." She motioned to the bed.

He started to remove his hand from her face. She grabbed his wrist, fingers circling the hard bones. She turned her face, pressing a desperate kiss to the center of his palm. Opening her mouth, she tasted his salty skin with her tongue.

He swallowed, his throat working, voice strangled. "It can't erase the last time."

"Last time wasn't . . . bad," she quickly asserted. Just desperate. Wild.

And there had been the fear, the overhanging threat that he could snap and possibly surrender to his hunger.

She shook her head. Maybe he was right and she did want to wipe out the memory of the first time. Who cared? It didn't change her wanting him, needing him right now.

"Just show me how it can be," she whispered. His eyes scanned her face for a long moment before he moved. Just a fraction. Indecision warred inside of him, his dark eyes gleaming.

Sweet torment. Craving.

Gratification curled through her. He wanted her. He could not resist.

Her heart hammered a violent tempo as his head dipped. His mouth was inches from hers when the explosion rocked the night.

They jumped apart, swinging to face the window,

staring out at the burst of red-gold against the city skyline.

"It's done," he murmured, and she sensed his concern. His fervent desire for the others to be safe. She prayed for the same. For all of them to be safe . . . especially Lily and Luc. They had probably saved her life, plucking her off the streets when they did.

She felt Sebastian turn, felt his stare on the side of her face as she gazed out at the city, at the great plume of smoke, several shades lighter than the night sky, twisting up between the crowded rooftops and domes of the ancient city.

"Ruby."

Her name fell like a hush in a churchyard. *Solemn. Sad.*

She faced him.

"Your eyes."

Her fingers flew to her cheek. "What—"

He shook his head. "They're the same."

Her heart constricted. The same. Silver, he meant. She was still a lycan. Gunter was not killed in the explosion.

Ruby turned to look out at the city. He was out there. Somewhere. "We'll never find him." *I'll be this way forever.*

All the relief she had felt, the exhilaration at knowing it would all end tonight vanished.

She took several steps away from Sebastian, the gulf between them back again. A yawning pit. Luc and Lily were able to live together, one as a lycan and one as a dovenatu, but Ruby did not kid herself. Sebastian wasn't Luc. And she wasn't Lily. They were not in love. Even if he lusted for her, she knew enough of men to know that desire was a fleeting emotion, and one they felt toward many women. It did not mean anything. She was a lycan. The very thing he spent a lifetime hunting and destroying. That's all that mattered now.

"We'll never find him," she said. "And I'll not stay here looking. I've had enough of this place."

She was going home. She knew enough to know that she could take precautions. Like Lily. Even without a husband to watch over her, she would manage. She would ask Adele to help.

"You can't hide from this, Ruby—"

"I know that," she snapped. "I'll live with it. At home. I'm used to dealing . . ." She swallowed. "With being different."

He shook his head in frustration. Irritation flowed from him into her. "And what happens at moonrise? You—"

"I'm not irresponsible," she snapped. "I'll take precautions."

His jaw clenched, that muscle flickering. "Don't

be stupid, Ruby. You can't handle this alone. You need—"

"Your Darius friend appears to manage."

"Darius is not my friend. But he has a full staff of employees at his disposal. And the experience you don't."

"I have friends." Well, just one she could count on for something like this. But she wasn't about to tell him that.

He laughed harshly, the sound grating. Contempt eddied through him. "You aren't thinking straight."

Her fist curled at her side, and she fought the urge to strike him, to knock the contempt free that he felt for her. "Maybe I'm not. Because I can't believe I actually wanted to *be* with you again." She flung a hand toward the door. "Get out."

With a hard nod, he moved to the door. "Fine. We'll finish this discussion tomorrow."

"So you can explain to me—again—how destroying lycans, me, is what you do? No, thanks."

Frustration simmered through her—part his, part hers. She followed him to the door. As soon as he passed through it, she slammed it after him.

Growling, she paced the room, kicking the leg of a chair. Damn him. He would never let her leave. He was too damn responsible to set her loose. He would keep her here hunting some damn lycan they probably could never catch . . . and all the time she would be at his mercy. How long before he gave up and just terminated her? It's what he did, after all. That much he had made clear.

A knock sounded at the door. She strode forward and yanked it open, expecting to see Sebastian again.

Only it wasn't him.

Angry words died on her lips as she stared into a pair of pewter eyes.

17

Jonah skidded to a halt before the smoldering rubble. Sirens sang in the distance. The building that had stood there moments ago was now only a pile of fire, smoke and debris.

His heart rose to his throat, strangling him as he choked through smoke thicker than fog. He shouted at the inferno, leaning forward with his whole body.

Only one person filled his head, only one person mattered as he stared at the snarling, twisting mass of fire. The only one he ever truly gave a damn about.

He shouted her name to the sky. "Sorcha!"

Sirens were upon him now. Tires screeched and he forced himself to move. He loped through the court-yard and vaulted up the side of one building. Effortlessly, he climbed until he sat on a rooftop. From his high perch, he watched, scanning the chaos below, telling himself maybe they survived. Sorcha. The other children. Even Ivo, crazed as he was. Jonah couldn't pretend that his loss didn't hurt, didn't affect him. Ivo had saved him as a boy.

But he had stayed all this time for one reason. One reason only. Sorcha.

Only lately he had contemplated breaking free of Ivo, venturing into the world on his own. To claim a normal life—even if it meant leaving a girl who looked at him with hero-worship in her eyes. Because he couldn't follow Ivo anymore. Because he couldn't stand witness as he broke his daughter.

Only this was not how he imagined it would end.

His hand fisted around the building's edge. *Sorcha.* Grief swelled over him. He'd seen the misery in her face tonight. And he had left her.

Sudden, new purpose filled him.

Someone would pay. He would make certain of that.

Cold certainty filled him. He didn't have to think very hard to arrive at the likely culprit for this carnage.

Who knew that a nest of lycans resided here?

Who might feel motivated to wipe them out?

The answer came to him with clarity. The hybrid that got away.

Before he'd escaped, Jonah read the rage in the dark-haired dovenatu's eyes. He knew his name—Sebastian Santiago. And he knew precisely how to find him. Ruby Deveraux of Beau Rivage, Louisiana. He knew all about her, courtesy of Gunter. Gunter had also related what he'd done to the pair of them. Reason enough for either one to want payback on the pack who tortured them. Not reason enough for Jonah to forgive what they had done. He closed his eyes. *Sorcha.*

His gut instinct told him that the dovenatu had not risked himself for the female to let her simply disappear from his life. No, if Jonah found the girl, he'd find Rafe Santiago, too.

Then he would have his revenge. *For Sorcha.*

Darius entered her hotel room without a word of invitation. He strolled toward the window with his hands clasped behind his back. A moment passed before Ruby shut the door. She watched him, keeping a careful distance, careful not to stray too close. Silly, she supposed. If he meant her harm, he would be on her in an instant. A few feet of separation wouldn't matter.

He stared out at the night for some moments, eyeing the serpent of smoke still rising into the sky.

"I see the mission was a success," she finally spoke into the silence, staring at his broad back.

"And I see you are unchanged," he returned.

She inhaled sharply against the unwelcome reminder. "Is that why you came here? To see if I was still a lycan."

"Yes." He didn't bother turning around. "And I cannot confess disappointment over the fact that you are yet one." He had an odd way of speaking, his manner of speech formal, hinting at an age lived and lost. A faint accent underlined his words.

He turned around then. If possible, the heat in those silver eyes blistered her. The range of his emotions hit her full blast and she staggered back a step, her hands moving behind her to curl around the edge of a table.

Desolation. Bleak as a sand-swept desert. As his gaze scanned her, she was assailed with a hungry need. *Yearning.* A deep need that had nothing to do with her specifically. He sought connection with another. With anyone who could fill the gnawing ache, and destroy his total sense of barren solitude, his isolation from the world and all in it.

"I'm not what you want," she announced.

His lips twisted and for a moment she thought he might smile : . . thought he might actually know how to smile. "How do you know what I want?"

"You're looking for a reason to live. It's not me."

His gaze flickered. She waited for his denial, his anger. The usual reaction when she read another's emotions and stripped them bare. Instead, he spoke. "I'm always too late."

"What do you mean?"

He shook his head. Jaw firming, he lifted his head and locked cool eyes on her. "I know you have developed feelings for Santiago, but don't fool yourself. He isn't going to save you. He won't even help you. It's done. You're a lycaness. All you can do is learn to cope. Every moonrise, you'll shift and feed unless—"

"I can sedate myself—"

"By yourself? It's far too tricky. What if you wake early? And all by yourself, you can't lock yourself away. Who would free you?"

"My best friend—"

"And who else? Who else can you rely on? She is mortal. What about when she dies? Or falls ill?"

All the questions Sebastian had posed.

He continued, "You need to have a fail-proof method in place."

"And I suppose you do?"

He nodded. "I have several safeguards in place. I won't risk setting myself loose on mankind." In a softer voice, he added, "Not again."

She hugged herself, hands chafing her arms. "How nice for you."

His expression turned annoyed. "I'm offering my resources to you."

Her gaze narrowed. "And what's the catch?"

"You and I would share those resources, naturally."

The skin of her face began to prickle. "Naturally."

"We share resources," he repeated. "We share everything."

Everything. His eyes swept over her then, and she understood his meaning perfectly. His next words made no mistake. "I was a monk once. Ages ago. I have no wish to be that again. I want a woman. A mate. A companion."

"And because I'm a lycan, it might as well be me?"

"I can't have a mortal. I won't. You're ideal."

She pressed a palm to her forehead. "This is insane."

"I'm promising you safety, the protection of your soul. Is sharing your life with me such a sacrifice?"

"Sharing our lives? You mean you get to . . . possess me." She shivered. "Sharing hints at equality. Freedom. Somehow this smacks of anything but that."

His silver gaze sparkled, and he closed the distance. One hand stole around her neck. His fingers pressed fiercely into her nape, forcing her to look up into his eyes. "Your soul does not mean much to you, then?" His nostrils flared. "Or you just crave that hybrid between your legs so much you can't stomach the thought of another, is that it? Let me assure you that I haven't had any complaints when it comes to that."

"I guess you've had a lot of practice over the years. Alongside all the killing you've done."

If possible, his silver eyes grew even chillier. Downright wintry. "That's right. I'm cursed, soulless. I've fed on innocents. So many I can't recount. I only remember their screams in my ears . . . their taste."

She shivered, closing her eyes. *Was this her future?*

He shook her, snapping her head back and forcing her eyes to reopen, to emerge from the bleak despair that threatened to pull her under.

"Listen to what I'm saying. Listen to what will happen to you if you don't take what I'm offering." He brought his face close, inhaling the skin at her throat as he spoke. "You reek of him. If you are his, then why is he not here? Why am I here? Making my claim?"

His words, his nearness, inflamed her. She felt an animal heat surge inside her. She recalled what Sebastian had said about lycans having an over-active libido.

Dangerously tempted to lean in, to surrender, she knocked his arms away from her with a speed she could scarcely fathom. Her voice puffed from her lips in an inhuman growl, "Never touch me. I'm not yours to claim. I belong to no one."

He smiled, his lips a cruel twist in his harshly handsome face. "Very well." He held both hands up in a disarming gesture. "I will never touch you again unless invited. Contrary to what you think, I am no beast. I can wait."

"You will wait forever," she proclaimed, shaking with outrage.

He inclined his head.

She watched as he moved toward the door, her breath still coming fast and hard. "We're pack creatures. We're not built for solitude."

Not built for solitude? But that was how she lived. All she knew. She couldn't risk anything else.

It was too much. She felt adrift, buffeted at every side with a barrage of unwanted emotions. Her heart leapt when he stopped and turned.

"I'll be leaving tonight. Without the others. It's a waxing moon, and I prefer to return home. We grow more aggressive as moonrise approaches. You may join me. I have a private jet. I'll take you wherever you wish to go. I imagine you would like to begin making your arrangements and preparing for moonrise yourself. Since that is what you have chosen."

She could leave tonight?

She could be in her own home, in her own bed

tomorrow, putting the memory of this entire nightmare behind her?

The offer was too tempting to refuse. Especially since she could sneak away without Sebastian even knowing. He'd be angry when he found out, but then he would forget about her. A part of him would probably be relieved that she had disappeared and lifted the responsibility of her from his shoulders.

As if he read her thoughts, Darius murmured, "This may be your only chance to get home. Santiago won't release you. If he doesn't find your alpha, who knows what he will do with you?"

She knew. And she shivered.

"No strings?" she blurted.

"No strings."

Her gaze narrowed, scanning every imposing inch of him from head to toe, but she felt no deception emanating from him, no foul purpose. "Why should you want to help me? In exchange for nothing?"

He shrugged one of his massive linebacker shoulders. "Perhaps I take cruel, perverse pleasure in keeping you out of Santiago's clutches. I have no great fondness for lycan hunters. Especially the ones that don't discriminate, which are most of them."

His lips curved slowly, the closest thing to a smile Ruby had seen on him. "I rather relish disappointing him. He wants you. I'm keeping him from having you. Bloody hybrid. They have it all. The gifts that go with being a lycan—in this case, I'll count you as a gift."

She stiffened.

He continued, "And none of the negatives. Like loss of soul, and the fact that innocent lives are in peril simply from my ungodly existence."

Unwilling to lecture him on why he should not begrudge Sebastian for simply being what he was, she strode to where she dropped her money belt, grateful that she had retained it—specifically her passport and visa—through all she had been through.

Securing it around her waist, she faced Darius and told herself she was doing the right thing. "Let's go."

18

Sebastian walked the streets, hands buried in his pockets, the myriad of smells and sounds doing nothing to distract him from the thought of Ruby, alone in her room. Alone. Afraid. A lycan.

They'd been through a lot together in a short time. He should turn himself around and march back into that hotel and give her a hard shake for even *thinking* he would destroy her. Destroy her as if she were any lycan he had come across in the course of his life. A depraved, soulless killing machine she was not, and how could she think he saw her that way?

He would not let her become that. Not even if he had to stand guard over her.

Didn't she know that?

She'd saved his soul in that room. He couldn't have continued as long as he had if not for her. With the heavy press of hunger on him, he'd felt a connection to her, and only that had staved off his descent to hell. Anyone else, and he would have broken.

She had given herself to him, deepening the connection so that he did not fall to the darkness that urged him to feed, to fulfill the gnawing ache clawing his insides. As though reminded of that hunger, he stopped and bought a *döner kebab* from a street side vendor. Taking a bite, he pushed on, the savory meat fueling him.

He'd give her the night, then he would sit her down and explain again why they needed to hunt down Gunter. Even if it took years, they would find him. Not that he believed it would take that long. Tracking was what he did. What he knew.

Finishing his last bite, he turned and headed back to the hotel. Conversations buzzed in the lobby, guests and staff alike milling about, speculating over the explosion across town. His keen hearing picked up words like *terrorist* and *insurgents*. Mankind was clueless about the darker forces at work, too busy creating their own conflicts and destroying themselves to notice otherworldly threats closing in.

At least after tonight, one such threat had been disposed. Ivo and his friends wouldn't be furthering their foul plan against humanity anymore.

Upon reaching his floor, he hesitated outside Ruby's room. No sound reached him. She probably slept. He lifted his hand to knock, then let it drop to his side.

Tomorrow would be soon enough. For now, he would let her sleep.

At eleven the following morning, Sebastian's patience came to an end.

He rose from a chair in the sitting area of Rafe's room, where his fingers had been tapping a heavy staccato on the arm. Their luggage sat near the door, waiting for their departure.

Kit and Rafe rose as one from the couch across from him, apparently reading his intention. "You sure you don't want to join us?"

"Ruby and I need to get on the trail before it grows cold."

Rafe drilled him with a knowing stare. "You have absolutely no idea what you're doing, do you?"

Gideon snorted from where he sat.

Sebastian inhaled deeply. "Yeah, I do. I'm keeping her alive. And making sure she doesn't hurt anyone in the process."

Rafe shook his head and brought his wife close to his side. He was always doing that. Touching her. Pulling her near him. As if he couldn't breathe without the feel of her against him. He'd never seen his brother like this. Happy.

"When will you visit us?" he asked. "Fishing's great this time of year." They lived in the small Texas town of Palacios, keeping a low profile since they had been targeted for elimination by NODEAL.

"Soon," he promised.

"Keep us informed, Seb."

Sebastian nodded.

Darius had left sometime in the night. Eager to be in his own home . . . and closer to his staff and steel-enforced room. One look at that hard-faced bastard and Sebastian felt only relief. Hunger brewed inside him. If that lycan ever broke loose, the world was in trouble.

He gave Rafe a quick hug before departing. He even hugged his sister-in-law. The little firecracker made Rafe happy. For that alone, he loved her.

As he shook March's hand, his thoughts drifted to Ruby. Several rooms over. His blood thickened in his veins, body tensing with eagerness.

Soon he was striding down the corridor. Rounding the corner, he paused. A housekeeping cart sat parked outside her room's door. Dread churned in his stomach. Shoving the cart aside, he stalked into the room. The maid squeaked and clutched a cleaning rag to her chest.

"Where is she?" he barked.

The woman shook her head wildly, and he cursed. Sweeping the empty room another look, he cursed again. He didn't need to interrogate the maid to learn the truth. The truth glared him straight in the face. Ruby was gone.

Sebastian inhaled. Only a faint whiff of her remained. She had left some time ago. Probably last night. Damn her.

He charged from the room and headed back down the hall. After several pounds of his fist on the door, Rafe opened it. Kit peered around her husband, her carry-on bag slung over her shoulder and sunglasses pushed back on her head.

"She's gone." He drove a hard line into the room, slamming the door behind him. "Left in the middle of the night. Can you believe it?" But the thing was . . . *he could*. When that building exploded and she hadn't reverted back, he'd seen the desolation in her face . . . her despair.

"What?" Rafe shook his head, clearly sharing his frustration. "Doesn't she want to hunt the alpha so she can break her curse—"

He snorted. "Apparently she doesn't put a lot of faith in that plan. Or me."

"Maybe you didn't give her a reason to stay," Kit suggested.

He glared at her. "What's that supposed to mean?"

Kit rolled her eyes. "C'mon, Sebastian. Anyone with eyes could see there's something between you two."

"So what?" Rafe snapped. "The woman shouldn't let her emotions get the best of her." Kit snorted, but he continued, waving a hand. "The moon's coming. She can't hide from it." He looked at Sebastian. "Where do you think she went?"

"I know where she went." Home. Where she usually hid from the world. He grimaced. She was accustomed to hiding what she was. This was only another reason for her to bury herself away.

Only Sebastian wouldn't let her.

"I know where she went. And I'm going to get her."

"She might not have gone home, if that's what you're thinking," March murmured.

Sebastian's head snapped in his direction, a dangerous churning starting in his gut. "What do you mean?"

"Darius left last night. Remember?"

He stared for a long moment at Gideon March, understanding sinking in. Rage erupted in his chest, spreading outward in a feral heat. The sensation grew, only burning hotter when he recalled Darius's interested gaze on Ruby time and time again last night. The beast clawed up from deep inside him.

"Get a hold of yourself," Rafe warned, watching

his face closely, no doubt seeing the evidence of his rage.

"She went with him," he muttered, her betrayal a hot knife to his flesh.

"You don't know that." Kit shot her brother a fuming *look-what-you-did* glare.

March shrugged. "He tried it with Claire when she was infected."

"Tried what?" Sebastian's fists flexed at his sides, bones stretching, bending, edging toward the beast. He took a deep breath, trying to regain control.

"When my wife was a newly turned lycan, Darius stole her from me. Tried to make her his mate—"

"I'll kill him," he announced.

March held a hand up in the air. "Now hold on. Claire wanted no part of him, so he let her go. He offered her the protection of himself . . . and his resources." He paused. "To someone scared and newly turned, that kind of guarantee of safety is tempting."

"You're saying she went with him to Houston? Willingly."

"*If* she even went with him," Rafe inserted, staring intently at Sebastian, trying to reach that part of him that threatened to spill over and consume him in a blistering burn. "This is all just speculation."

He clenched his jaw and gave a tight nod. "Well, let's make it fact, then."

Rafe settled back on his heels. "You'll go to the States."

"First Louisiana, then Houston." He hoped he found her at her home, but either way he was beyond pissed. And he was going to let her know it.

Kit shook her head. "Looking at you right now—" She broke off with a sigh and dragged a hand through her hair, ruffling the dark blond strands. "Hell, I feel sorry for her."

"Yeah?" he bit out. "Well, don't. She chose her path."

And he would make certain she regretted it.

"Thanks for picking me up," Ruby said as she slid inside the front passenger seat to a welcome blast of air conditioning. Relieved to be home, she couldn't help smiling. Buckling her seat belt, several moments passed before she realized the car hadn't pulled away from the curb.

As jets swooshed overhead, she turned to face Adele and felt her smile falter. Never had she seen her friend look so furious. Her gray eyes glittered, and her knuckles clenched white where they gripped the steering wheel.

"I thought you were dead," she bit out.

A shuttle van honked behind them and Ruby motioned weakly for them to drive. "Shouldn't you go?"

Adele yanked the car into drive. Ruby winced.

"I oughta kick your ass to the curb, Ruby Deveraux! The nerve of you calling me an hour ago with an *I'm back! Can you pick me up?*" Her thumb began a furious beat on the steering wheel as they left the Lafayette airport behind.

"*Dead.* Do you hear me? That's what Rosemary told me to expect when you left the hotel looking for some girls who ran off. That was over a week ago!" She stopped at a red light, shaking her head. Her abundance of russet-brown hair tossed against her shoulders. Truly wild hair. Some strands curly, some just wavy, some frizz. Even a few pieces fell straight. "Do you know what I've been through?"

Ruby's voice fell soft, regretful. "No." She'd been too busy surviving to consider how her disappearance may have affected Adele.

The light turned green, and Adele gunned her hatchback as fast as it could go. Ruby's head slammed back on the headrest.

"Take it easy."

"Easy? Easy? Where the hell have you been? Rosemary has been no help whatsoever. I started to wonder if she had something to do with it. Maybe she sold you into a white slave ring or something."

Ruby laughed. She couldn't help it. Then the thought of all she had been through hit her and her laughter died an abrupt death. The reality of the last weeks seemed even less probable than being sold into white slavery. And she needed to explain the truth to Adele. Every incredible, implausible detail. When she could hardly believe it all herself.

Back on American soil, Istanbul—*Sebastian*—seemed a lifetime ago. By now he would have woken, would have realized she'd left during the night. And likely with whom. The thought made her stomach knot.

Darius had been true to his word. He kept to his seat on his side of the plane, never even engaging her in conversation. Except when they landed. Then the dark-haired lycan had shoved his card into her hand and told her she could count on him should she change her mind. Strangely, it gave her some comfort. Until she remembered that taking his protection meant taking him as a mate. She was certain that caveat hadn't changed.

"I understand your anger. Let's just wait until we're home and then I'll explain everything." She would hate for Adele to run off the road. She'd always been an emotional driver—she had always been emotional—and this would likely send her into a ditch.

"Fine," Adele grumbled. "I didn't let Rosemary know you're home, but you're going to have to call her. She's in a real temper. Her supervisor is expected home any day. He flew over there to work with the local police as they investigated the girls' disappearance." Adele lifted a hand and made quotation marks with her fingers at the word investigation.

That Adele did not include her in the mention of an investigation did not surprise her. The girls were minors. More focus would fall on them than a missing adult. Not that Ruby expected much of a search to continue for the girls either. Not without parents pressuring from home. Her throat tightened. Soon they would be forgotten. Two files in some foreign office. Lives lost, histories never told, never known. Bleakness filled her heart.

"I'll call tomorrow and let them know I'm back."

Adele sent her a sly glance before looking out the front windshield again. Ruby knew she sounded ambivalent, which she wasn't. Far from it. She simply knew the girls were dead. What good would it do to call Rosemary and have her rush over with a barrage of questions that would serve no purpose now?

Almost an hour later, they pulled up in front of Ruby's old farmhouse. Her Corolla sat beneath the two-vehicle carport she'd put up last year. Two-vehicle. As if she had been holding out hope for another soul to take up residence with her.

She sat in the car for a long moment, staring at the house through the window. It looked smaller. A forlorn shape beneath draping cypresses and sycamores. The once-cheery yellow paint had faded more than she realized. So much that the house she loved, that she clung to like a life raft, looked dingy.

She remembered when her mother painted the house. It had been one of those projects she created following an *incident*. Her projects would take her mind off whatever happened, let her pretend it had not occurred, keeping her preoccupied, away from Ruby for a spell. Until she got over it.

The time her mother painted the house, it involved Ruby's refusal to spend the night with Ritabeth, the Methodist preacher's daughter. When Momma asked why, Ruby told her that Ritabeth didn't really like her. That Ritabeth's daddy had the hots for Momma and made his daughter invite Ruby for a sleepover. Just so he could see Momma. Of course, all this she had gleaned through her *gift*. Momma understood that at once.

Soon after, Momma stopped asking questions that began with *why*. Around that time, she just gave up. Period. When she died two years later, Ruby felt her relief as she drew her last sip of breath. Even Momma turned out not so very different than her father. Her method of escape just differed from his.

"Getting out?" Adele's question snapped her to attention.

Nodding, she stepped from the car and walked to the front porch. Adele, who had kept her keys for safekeeping, handed them to her. Unlocking the door, she stepped inside.

The house smelled musty, airless. She dropped her keys on the table near the door and made a beeline for her couch. A refuge of sorts. She had spent many a night there, both with Adele and without, a pint of Ben and Jerry's in her lap, watching movies. The old ones were her favorites. Jimmy Stewart movies. *Shenandoah, Rear Window, It's a Wonderful Life.* Dropping onto the worn cushions, she kicked off her shoes and curled her feet beneath her.

"All right." Adele dropped on the loveseat. Perfect breasts pushed against her bright orange tank top where the words BEACH OR BUST were written. She curled her legs on the couch, her pink flowy skirt draping artfully without the slightest effort. With her Heidi Klum body, she had guys calling for a date every night. "Dish. And what's with the freaky contacts?"

Hopefully, Adele would accept what Ruby was about to tell her. Adele knew the extraordinary existed. They never discussed the extent of Ruby's abilities, but Adele knew. Accepted.

"So," she began, clearing her throat. "Have you ever heard the word *lycan* before?"

19

The night hummed outside her window. Alive in a way she had never noticed before and her new animal self felt acutely linked to. Even the trees outside her window seemed to breathe, leaves rustling, life pulsing deep beneath the bark.

Ruby moved from the window, setting her alarm to seven. She would prefer not setting it at all, but she needed to resume life, and that meant facing the day bright and early. After Adele left, she'd gone into town and bought groceries—enough for herself and enough to get back into the swing of work.

At the top of tomorrow's list: a call to Rosemary. Her second goal came as the result of her long, exhausting conversation with Adele. After explaining everything, Adele had promised her support and the two of them put their heads together, trying to figure out how they were going to cope with the coming full moon.

Adele's cousin seemed the natural solution. A pharmacy school drop-out, Dwayne's abuse and marketing of prescription drugs was widely known throughout the parish. Suddenly his criminal activities were to their benefit. When they began contemplating how to get their hands on sedatives, his name was the first on their lips.

Sighing, she stretched. Her sheets felt good, the cool, crisp cotton a welcome chill against her bare legs. Even with the air conditioner running a steady purr, the old house never got too cool, baking all day in the wet heat. She laced her fingers over her stomach and stared into the dark. In her mind, she calculated the time in Turkey. What was Sebastian doing? Was he still there? An unwanted throb started in the core of her at the thought of him. He could have gone to any one of his apartments. She supposed none really qualified as a home. But with his nomadic existence, he didn't require one. Without her as a rock about his neck, he had probably returned to his hunting.

She thought about how intensely she had wanted—needed—to return here, to reach home, refuge. She did not have much in the way of people, but she had this house.

Sebastian didn't have that. Nor did he seem to want it—to want anything or anyone. It only reminded her of their differences and confirmed in her mind that leaving was for the best.

She closed her eyes, commanding herself to sleep. To forget. *To forget him.*

The world outside hummed and pulsed in rhythm to her heart, a primeval symphony. Soon her breathing fell soft, even and regular with that world. And she drifted off to sleep.

She woke with sudden alertness, pouncing up on all fours on the bed. The old mattress's springs gave the barest squeak. She held herself still, head cocked to the side, listening to the night, to the humming world outside, the barely perceptible sounds of her house settling its old bones. Nothing.

She didn't hear anything, but she knew. She felt.

She wasn't alone. Someone else was here. Close.

She vaulted off the bed and landed on the floor, silent as a cat on the balls of her feet. But she didn't have time to marvel at her agility. Using every one of her newly developed senses, she slipped from her room.

Soundless as the breath of death, she slid along the hall's wall, close as plaster, palms skimming. Not a sound rose on the air and yet every hair on her body stood on end, tingling and vibrating with awareness. Her fingers stretched against the wall, then flexed into a curling fist.

Even with her light tread, the bottom step on the stair creaked as it always did. She winced, waiting for someone to dart out from behind a piece of furniture.

Nothing.

She released the breath she had been holding and continued, eyes peering easily through the darkened house, missing nothing.

She froze. Her scalp tightening, tingling. Her heart rate accelerated in her too-tight chest. A strong current of emotion slammed into her. *Fury. Exhilaration*. She looked up at the precise moment a figure dropped down from the air, landing in front of her.

She reacted. Didn't think.

Without a sound, her hand lashed out, striking the intruder in the face. She registered the crunch of bone against her hand. Shocked at the speed of her reflexes and her own strength, she hesitated. Just a second of pause. A second too long.

She pulled her arm back for a second blow, but she never had the chance to unleash it.

A hard fist closed around her own hand. She tugged. Winced at the crushing force tightening around her fingers. He was strong. Stronger than her. *Not human.*

Panting, her gaze traveled from the large hand holding her fist hostage to the face in front of her. *Sebastian.* He stared at her, all hard, unforgiving angles, his chilled stare striking coldness in her heart.

"Coming into your own, I see," he murmured, voice softly even, unsettling given the rage glittering in his eyes. His wrath cut through her, bitter as poison, and she knew she had to flee, had to save herself. She'd never felt such fury from him before. Not even when he fought lycans. This was personal.

"Where's Darius?" he demanded.

"What?"

Her gaze flicked away, searching, hunting for a way out, away from him, from what he would do to her. He had not flown halfway around the world to save her. She wasn't that naïve. If he'd come all this way, it was to finish this. *Finish her.*

"Darius," he ground out, his gaze sweeping her from head to toe. "Is he here?"

She looked down at herself, at her cotton night-gown that fell just above her knees. She crossed her arms over her chest, the gesture defensive and self-conscious. He made her feel that way. Young and awkward. Made her remember this was the man who had taken her virginity with a savagery that should have horrified her . . . instead of leaving her aching, wanting more even now.

His voice cracked on the air, making her jump. "Where is he?"

She tried to speak. "What are—"

He hauled her close, crushing her fist between their bodies. His other hand dug cruelly into the back of her neck, forcing her still. He inhaled against her neck, his face pressed hotly into her throat. She gasped. *Wanting. Stark possessiveness.*

Her body instantly reacted, responded to his in a mortifying flood of heat. "Did he have you?"

She shook her head. "No. Of course not. Why would he—"

"You left with him," he announced flatly, a deadness entering his eyes, a contradiction to the flood of emotions tearing through him. *Tearing through her.*

"That doesn't mean I'm with him now. He dropped me at the airport and then left. End of story."

He stared at her, some of his tension lessening, but none of the anger. None of the resentment. He wanted to punish her. Hurt her. Anger still clawed through him. And more than that. *Dark need. Hot desire.* A hard ridge pressed into her belly. His hand dropped from her neck and cupped her ass, gripping it and lifting her against him. Moistness wet her panties. Her limbs grew heavy, molten, a clenching sensation starting low in her belly. *God. Oh, God. Oh, God . . .*

And she knew. Knew she had to run. Escape.

Now was her moment. Now or never.

"Can I get dressed?" she asked, having no idea if he would allow it.

He angled his head and considered her. The rage was there, dark and dangerous, a live pulsing thing on the air. "Why? I'm a heartbeat away from ripping your clothes off."

She sucked in a sharp breath. "Oh. Is that how it's going to be?"

He forced her hand down, pressing it over the hard length of him. "It's how it has to be."

She exhaled and did her best to sound enticing when adrenaline burned through her veins. "Then let's go upstairs."

He stared at her for a long moment, unblinking.

"A bed would be a welcome change," she added, trying to sound tempting, going for coy. Her voice shook.

With a hard nod, he released her.

She turned and took the first step. Shooting a cautious look over her shoulder, she advanced several more. She knew he had to hear her heart pounding against her ribs and hoped he credited it to arousal and not her anxiety over what she was about to do.

Halfway up the stairs, she took a bracing breath and swung. With a grunt, she kicked him square in the chest with the flat of her foot. As hard as she could.

He flew off the stairs and through the air like a missile, striking the front door. She didn't wait for him to rise. Didn't wait to see if he was okay.

She turned and ran. Fire in her limbs. Heart rising to her throat. A prayer on her lips that he not catch her—not kill her.

In her room, she slammed the door behind her and rushed to her window. She flung it up and punched the screen free. Swinging one leg over the ledge, she vaulted onto the roof, sliding over the shingles.

The neighbor's farm was only a couple of miles if she cut through the woods. Mr. Wilson would lend her his truck to get to Adele's place. He was one of the few people who didn't mutter *freak* beneath his breath when she walked past.

She dropped to the ground, not feeling the slightest jar to her body. She landed lightly on her feet . . . like brushing the bottom of a swimming pool. And she was off.

She took to the woods, warm wind rushing over her, tangling in her hair, the humming trees a blur in the night. Her bare feet flew over the ground, not feeling a twig or root.

A small light flickered ahead. A porch light. She was almost to the farm. Elation filled her. Soon the trees would clear and she would be at Mr. Wilson's fence.

A shape surged from the trees like night coming to life, stepping in front of her. Dark eyes, light flashing in the centers . . . and she knew. She had not escaped. As fast as she moved, he moved faster. Tears of defeat stung her eyes.

Her arms flailed, as if swimming a backstroke to avoid him.

He stretched out a hand to catch her.

"No!"

He seized both her arms and hauled her until their noses nearly touched. "What the hell is wrong with you? When are you going to stop running? You should know that you can't escape me." He smiled cruelly, a jagged twisted movement of his lips. "Sweetheart, you might be a lycan now, but I've been at this game a hell of a lot longer than you. I can catch you with my eyes closed."

She struggled, whimpering like captured prey, remembering only his vow to destroy all lycans—her.

"Ruby," he growled, his voice thickening in that way that alerted her of his descent to darkness. Even if she hadn't heard it, she would know. Would remember from that endless stretch of time with him in their bleak little prison.

Rage. Deadly and so tightly strung. He was ready to snap, erupt. He would turn, change into that thing that could so easily tear her apart. Only this time, he would feel justified in doing so. Because she was a creature that needed slaying. For the sake of mankind.

His hands on her didn't budge.

Closing her eyes, she stopped struggling. She just . . . stopped.

She couldn't beat him.

"Just make it quick." The words slipped from her lips in a hushed rush.

"*What?*"

Bewilderment. Confusion.

She felt his frustration heighten and she rushed to clarify, "I know you don't relish this. You think you have to do it . . . so do it."

At least my soul will be safe. There was that to appreciate.

"You little fool." His rage grew to a burning sear.

She hissed, the heat of it singeing her. She strained against his grip.

"You think I've come all this way to destroy you?"

"How likely is it we will find Gunter?" She shook

her head. "You said yourself that you kill lycans. Hunt them down like dogs. That's *what* you do."

"But I wasn't talking about you!"

He shook her slightly, dark, glowing eyes scanning her face. "Is that what you think of me? You probably saved my life, my soul at least, in that dungeon. And you think I would just destroy you?"

She opened her mouth, trying to explain that was what she *felt* from him. Even now. *Rage. Conflict. Frustration.* Feelings so intense and frightening she had to run. What else could any of it mean except that he was torn by his duty to destroy her?

"I feel you," she whispered. "I feel everything you feel."

His expression turned stoic. "Is that a fact?"

"Yes." He knew it. She had not forgotten the way he turned from her when she told him she was an empath. "It sucks, but it lets me know things." She thrust out her chin. "Like how you feel about me."

A shutter fell over his eyes. "Oh, yeah? Well, then you don't interpret emotions very well."

She scowled. "Of course, I—"

"You might feel what I feel, but you don't understand what any of it means if you think I'm out to kill you," he bit out.

She angled her head, watching him warily. "I feel your rage—"

He hauled her against his chest. "Maybe I'm furious at myself? Furious and filled with a killing rage for wanting this when I've already taken from you what I had no right to take?"

He kissed her then, his mouth hot, hungry and thorough, forcing her lips open for him. And like last time, his passion ran over. *Blistering lust*. Consuming her until she couldn't identify her feelings from his. They were one and the same. She tasted her own desire on his lips.

This was not the kiss of someone bent on killing her. That much she knew. She didn't know what he was to her anymore, but she knew right now that she needed this. Needed him.

He broke their kiss, his gaze scanning her face, heat erupting everywhere he looked. *Desire*. "No one is forcing us together right now. I've no excuse for doing this—"

"It wasn't force then," she uttered with absolute conviction, her blood a desperate burn in her veins. "It isn't now."

Tugging his head back down, she kissed him with all the dark need running rampant inside her.

Still kissing, they dropped to the ground, grass and twigs crackling beneath their bodies. Ruby had thought she wanted tenderness, wanted sweet, gentle lovemaking like she had fantasized about—before she knew what desire really felt like. But this fever couldn't be slowed, couldn't follow an easy pace.

Muttering about the uncomfortable ground, he settled on his back and splayed her body over his. The night sang around them, heavy with locusts and the rustling of small animals in the thick undergrowth. Their lips never broke as their clothes dropped away. Her hands trailed over every inch of him, following the hard lines and ridges, seeing him perfectly in the dark.

A scar puckered the flesh of one shoulder. She hadn't noticed it before in the darkness of their prison. She traced it with one hand, following its winding path over his shoulder and descent down his back.

"I thought you regenerated."

"That happened before I turned. An accident when I tried to clear the blades of a plow." The rough rasp of his voice scraped the air. Goosebumps broke out over her flesh.

He caught her hand and brought it back to his chest. She felt the deep thud of his heart beneath her palm, beneath the smooth, supple texture of his skin.

He dark eyes gleamed. "I've never wanted a woman the way I want you."

"I'm not a woman anymore," she dared to remind,

moistening her lips. "Not that I've ever been . . . normal, Sebastian. Even before . . ."

His lips twisted. "Are you trying to scare me off? Look who you're talking to. 'Normal' isn't me."

A heartbeat passed. The light at the centers of his eyes grew. Fire in the night. "Whatever you are, Ruby Deveraux, I want you. Not to hunt you. Or hurt you. But you. All of you."

20

The ground and trees pulsed around them, humming, watching, listening. *I want you.* The words echoed in her head. It wasn't the tender love-making Ruby imagined for herself should she ever come together with a man again. Only he wasn't *just* a man. And she had already accepted how far from ordinary she was.

Their joining was just as wild and violent as the last time. Only this time, it couldn't be blamed on Sebastian. No dark animal hunger drove him, frightening her in its force.

Straddling him, she sank over him, kissing him deeply. Her hand delved between them, closing around his satin hardness. He swelled in her hand. Groaning in her mouth, his tongue tangled with hers. She wiggled over him, teasing the head of him against her opening.

"Ruby," he hissed, surging his hips upward and driving into her.

Her cry floated up to the trees. She arched her spine and ground down against him, seating herself fully, needing, craving closeness, to have him deeper.

The moon gleamed silver through the latticework of branches, watching, feeding her soul.

His hands lifted to her breasts, the callused pads of his palms rasping her tender flesh. Her nipples grew hard, sensitive, aching against his palms.

Ripples of pleasure eddied out from between her legs to every nerve ending in her body. His hands clasped her waist, lifting and lowering her over him. Again. And again. A deep moan built inside her throat at the drag of his flesh against her, inside her . . . at the hot flex of his hands on her breasts. Her head fell back as the torment grew, spiraling and twisting tighter and tighter between her legs.

Twigs and bramble caught in the ends of her hair trailing to the ground, but she couldn't care, couldn't stop quivering, trembling atop him as he drove into her. Harder. Faster. Deeper.

In the silvery glow of moonlight, she saw his face contort, blur in and out as the beast in him overcame the man. Only it didn't horrify her. She opened herself, let her own demon beast take him deeper, take her farther, where the darkest of her cravings lurked.

She screamed his name, violent heat erupting through her as she burst. Her nails scored his shoulders until the faint fragrance of blood filled her nostrils.

Birds squawked and flew from their nests with shuddering wings at her savage cry, their sleep shattered. Half-blind with her orgasm, she watched them soar through the branches, dark smudges on the night. To her passion-blurred vision, it seemed they rose directly to the moon. The source of it all.

All her life she had fought emotions. The feelings of others. But in doing so, she had numbed herself to feeling her own heart.

Never had she lost herself like this. Lost herself to . . . *herself*. That gleaming moon brought out more than her feral nature. It brought out . . . *her*.

His release shuddered through her. She smoothed her palms over his shoulders, gentling her touch now that her blood pumped less fiercely. The slick skin of his body rippled and flexed under her hands. She felt his sense of gratification shared in it. He pulled back, his dark eyes with that flame writhing in the center gazed at her, looking at her. Seeing her. And she let him. For once, she didn't want to run, to hide. *Tenderness.*

Rising, he pulled her to her feet and helped her

dress. Through the trees, the lights of Mr. Wilson's farmhouse flickered. She turned her back on it. Her hand in Sebastian's, they walked home together.

Sebastian woke with a languorous stretch, sated as a well-fed cat beneath the jungle sun. His hand felt beside him, finding that side of the bed bare, only the faint indentation on the pillow indicating Ruby had been there.

Lifting his head, his gaze swept the room, appreciating it in the light of day. It was feminine, the soft blue paint soothing, furniture well-worn, antiques. Mismatched pieces that worked well together in the room.

Throwing back the floral-patterned comforter, he rose from the bed and slid on his jeans, for once not worried over Ruby's whereabouts. He sensed her movements downstairs. Felt the steady pulse of her heart. Smelled the breakfast she cooked. Bacon. Eggs. Butter melting on warm toast.

His lips twisted as he made his way barefoot to the stairs, the old house's wood floor creaking beneath his feet. A cabinet shut in the kitchen below over the sound of faint humming. He shook his head. So domestic. He'd be lucky to find a box of crackers in any one of his flats.

He would not have imagined himself in such a

setting. With such a woman. *Not a woman,* a voice whispered in his head. A lycan. His smile slipped. Heaviness weighed his chest. *Yes, there was still that.*

The phone rang as he was halfway down the stairs. Ruby hurried from the kitchen, crossing in front of the stairs. He devoured the sight of her. The loose flow of her hair, a dark rich brown against her white blouse. She wore a loose skirt. Her feet were bare, the nails pink and shiny. Again, he was struck with the domesticity of it all. Of her. This house. A home, he realized with a jolt. The one thing he had never possessed. He'd come close those years with Rafe and his mother. Only it was hard to ever feel at home with a mother who stood over your bed with a knife in her hand. Suddenly, he better understood Ruby's need to come back here.

She spoke into one of those old rotary phones with the twisted cord.

"I know, I know . . . I was going to call you this morning . . ." A longer silence fell.

"Yes, I understand you, but I only got back yesterday."

A certain thickness entered her voice. He took the last few steps. She looked up as he stopped beside her. Standing this close, he could smell the cinnamon and sugar on her. His stomach growled . . . and not just for food.

"Yes," she murmured into the mouthpiece. "Fine. I'll be here. See you then."

When she lifted the phone from her ear, he took it and returned it to its home.

They stared at one another for a long moment. His heart beat hard in his chest, filling his ears.

"Hi," she murmured, her voice a soft little breath that touched something deep inside him.

Without responding, he gathered two fistfuls of her skirt, bunching the fabric at her waist, looking at her intensely, drinking the sight of her.

"What—" Her words died when he slipped a hand beneath the edge of her panties. Finding her wet, he played with her slick folds, gliding a finger against her opening.

"Oh, God," she cried when he exerted more pressure, easing that finger inside her. She clung to him, her body familiar and achingly sweet, her nails scoring his biceps. He kissed her long and deep.

Unable to wait, he folded an arm around her waist and lifted her. She moved forward eagerly, wrapping her legs around him. He locked gazes with her as he worked open his zipper and freed himself, wondering if she felt what he was feeling right now.

He entered her with a hard thrust. Groaning, he claimed her lips, swallowing her small cries as he pumped between her trembling thighs.

It wasn't supposed to be like this. This good. This . . . everything. It never had been before.

Only she doesn't know that. You're her first. She probably thinks sex is this intense every time.

Part of him rebelled at that thought, wanting her to know that what they had was unparalleled, nothing she would ever find with another man. The other part of him knew it was for the best if she thought she could get this anywhere . . . with anyone. That way it wouldn't crush her when he moved on. As he naturally would.

The thought fueled him with fury, made him work in and out of her harder, his hand clutching her ass in a bloodless grip. The beast rose in him, intent on possessing her so that she would never forget this—*him*.

She clung to him, crying out her own release the moment before he reached his. He clutched her close, staggering a bit, shudders shaking him. Her legs still wrapped around him, he looked down into her flushed face, drowning in her probing gaze, unnerved at the knowledge that he could hide nothing from this woman. Even if her interpretation was sometimes off, she felt everything he felt.

Alarming. Terrifying. Because what he felt right now was that in this moment, in this room, with this woman . . . he had found what he never knew he wanted, but what he had been running toward all his life.

He cleared his throat. "I'm sorry. I had meant to start with a simple 'good morning' when I came downstairs."

A smile shook her lips.

"Did I hurt you?" He brushed a thumb against her cheek. She'd been hurt too many times since they first met. He didn't want to heap any more pain on her. She'd felt enough of that lately.

"You didn't hurt me." Her smile deepened. "I've learned that I am quite resilient."

Yes. Staring into her pewter eyes, he wondered how he could have forgotten that. Those were eyes he had hunted for as long as he could remember. Eyes he had watched fade to mortal shades following the death shots he delivered.

A sound emerged, low in the distance. "Someone's coming," he growled.

Ruby slid her legs to the floor and darted to the front door, peering out through the curtains. "I don't see anyone—"

"Listen." He tucked himself back in his jeans. "You'll see soon enough."

She cocked her head to the side, gaze shifting, flitting about as she listened. "You're right. I hear a car."

Several more moments passed. Sebastian moved to stand beside her. "Are you expecting anyone?"

She shook her head. "No. Later—"

"There," he cut in as the gleaming hood of a car cleared the trees that crowded the end of her dirt driveway.

"Oh. It's Adele. My friend." She straightened, shifting on her feet, frowning at him. "Maybe you should go upstairs."

"You want to hide me from your friend?"

"Just—"

"Have you told her what happened to you in Istanbul?"

"Yes."

The skin of his face tightened. Whatever she had said about Sebastian must not have been good if she wanted him to hide. It wouldn't be the first time. His mother had treated him like a dirty little secret—her shame.

Ruby waved a hand. "Just until I explain you—"

"No problem." Turning, he marched up the steps.

"Give me a few moments and I'll get rid of her. I made breakfast. You must be hungry—"

He continued, not looking back.

"Sebastian," she called, but he didn't stop. He walked until he was in her bedroom. Once there, he looked around, trying not to inhale the scent of sex emanating from the bed. Dragging a hand through his hair, he wondered what the hell he was doing with Ruby Deveraux.

21

"He's *here*?" Adele lifted her gaze to the ceiling, then dropped her voice to a whisper. "What's he doing here? Why haven't you called the cops on his ass?"

Ruby smiled, despite how much she didn't feel like it. Sebastian was up there, angry with her. And she wasn't quite sure why. "You don't need to whisper, Adele. He can probably hear you anyway."

The color bled from her friend's face. She looked up at the ceiling again, big hair tossing as she dropped her head back.

"And no, we shouldn't call the police. What would I tell them? I have a half-breed lycan in my bedroom? Oh, and I'm one, too, by the way. Well, worse. I'm a full lycan, so don't come ringing my doorbell when the moon's full or I might—"

"Whoa, back up." Adele waved a hand, palm up, fingers splayed wide. "He's in your bedroom? What's that about? Guest room too small?" She arched a brow and crossed her arms over the large breasts pushing against her tight purple tee. "Did you forget to mention any other details about when you were in Istanbul?"

Ruby bit her lip. Maybe a small detail. Like losing her virginity. Lying would be pointless. Even if telling heat did not sweep her face, Adele could always sniff out when Ruby was less than honest. Inhaling, Ruby looked her squarely in the eyes and let her read what truth she would.

"You did not!" Adele tossed her handbag to the floor and propped her hands on her waist. "All these years you held out, and then you just give it up to him?"

"Don't get mad. You're the one who always told me I put too much importance on sex. That I should just do it and—"

"You've known this guy for how long? What happened to all that talk of holding out for someone special?"

She swallowed, stopping herself from declaring

that it *was* special . . . that it had been special. That being with Sebastian felt right. And more than that. It was a compulsion she couldn't resist. But with Sebastian upstairs, she didn't dare say any of that.

Adele shook her head. "What a hypocrite."

Adele's disappointed gaze hurt. Which, in turn, angered Ruby. "At least I don't give it up to just any guy."

Adele pulled back, inhaling sharply. "Meaning, I do?" Over her anger, Ruby picked up her hurt. "At least I'm out there living, enjoying my life instead of hiding. And last time I checked, the guys I take to bed are human."

Ruby flinched. "I don't need you judging me right now."

"Right." Adele snatched up her purse and dug through the contents. "You just need me when I can do something for you." She slammed a box of syringes and a couple vials of liquid on the side table beside the couch. "According to Dwayne, it takes about thirty minutes to go into effect after injection." She marched toward the door and pulled it open. "Call me when your friend leaves and you need me again. I'm a slut, remember? I'm good at being used."

"Adele." Ruby stretched out her hand but she was already out the door.

She moved into her living room and dropped down on the sofa. Shaking her head, she lowered her face into her hands. "Shit."

"That was quick." Between her fingers, she spied Sebastian's feet stepping in front of her.

She lowered her hands. "Not my best moment."

"Yeah, well. Personalities have been known to change after infection . . . boldness and aggression come hand in hand with being a lycan."

"I guess calling my best friend a slut is . . . bold."

Sebastian picked the bottle of pills off the table. "What's this?"

"Sedatives." She smiled without humor. "I told you I would look after myself. That I have friends who can help me."

"Your friend is a doctor?"

"No. Her cousin's a pill pusher."

"A pharmacist?"

"No. Dwayne doesn't exactly have a license."

His dark brows pulled together. "You went to some drug dealer?"

Ruby pushed to her feet. "I couldn't exactly go to a doctor and get a prescription." She stalked past him, stopping at the stairs. "I didn't think someone who spends his life killing could be such a moral prig."

"Ruby." He spoke her name as if striving for patience. She felt his frustration . . . his disappointment.

Fantastic. Apparently she was all about disappointing those close to her this morning. "The less people who know about you the better—"

"She didn't tell Dwayne what it—"

"So he's just wondering why he gave you enough to knock out a horse. You don't think he'll mention that to someone else when he's chatting it up in a bar one night? What if he gets busted? What if he rats out all his customers and suppliers . . . *you*."

Ruby blinked. She hadn't considered that.

"Dwayne won't talk." She curled a hand around the railing. "Look, I didn't ask for you to come here. And I didn't ask for your advice."

He strode across the living room. "Regardless, I'm here. And I'm staying through moonrise to make sure you can handle all this as you claim." His voice dripped skepticism.

"And if you think I can't?"

"I'm taking you back to Turkey. To pick up Gunter's trail."

She made a sound of disgust. A trail long cold by now. Fire burned in her chest at the thought of leaving home again. Of diving back into the world that had shown her nothing but cruelty and brutality. "I won't go."

"Yes," the word fell hard, clipped. His eyes glinted. "You will."

"So what are you going to do? Babysit me for the rest of my days? You really want to be stuck together that long?" Her chest heaved, and she regretted the question the instant it dropped from her mouth. She sounded needy, like she was fishing for a commitment from the guy.

A muscle in his jaw flexed wildly. "That would suck, wouldn't it?"

Her brows pulled together. He emitted bitterness. *Anger. Mockery.*

He continued. "You insist you can handle this? Then prove it. Then I'll leave." He swung around into the kitchen. A plate rattled and she knew he was helping himself to the breakfast she had prepared. She had made it with him in mind . . . the memory of their night in every whisk, every seasoning sprinkled. Now all that seemed a long time ago. Even their quick coupling in the living room seemed to belong to some other time, some other people.

Prove it.

She would. The sooner she proved it to him, the sooner he would leave her alone. She just had to endure him until moonrise and not make a fool of herself by revealing how much he affected her. To distance herself while living with him beneath her roof. How hard could it be?

Weathering life alone was what she knew. What she did.

Rosemary marched into the living room, a wicker purse with neon pink and yellow flowers swinging from her arm. A Beau Rivage deputy sheriff followed close behind. "Well, Ruby Deveraux, where are the girls?"

"Have a seat." Ruby gestured to the couch. "Can I get you a drink?"

"This is serious business. You could be in big trouble here," Rosemary cut in before the deputy could accept Ruby's offer, which he looked inclined to do. Mouth pursing, he shook his head. Regretfully.

"*I'm* in trouble?" Ruby lowered into the sofa chair, her favorite. She had sat through many a *Top Chef* marathon in its cushioned depths, a plate of stuffed jalapeños on her lap. "What have I done?"

"You ran off with the girls—"

"What? *They* ran off. I went looking for them," she clarified. "Remember?"

The deputy took out his notepad and began scribbling in it. "That so? Ms. LeMoine here claims you left with them—"

"She knows that's not true. She's the one who told me they snuck off to attend some party. I went in search of them."

"Well, you didn't expect me to go!" the social worker exclaimed.

The deputy frowned. "So you concur that Ms. Deveraux did not leave the hotel with the girls?"

Rosemary pressed her lips tight, splotches of color breaking out over her pudgy cheeks. Her nostrils flared wide. "Y-yes. I do recall that."

The man released a heavy sigh, and lifted his gaze from his notepad, settling his eyes on Ruby. "And did you locate the girls?"

She shifted on her feet. "I never found them. But I'm fine though," Ruby said tightly, flicking an angry glare to both of them. "Thank you for asking."

"Oh, you always were one to land on your feet." Rosemary nodded. "I told Deputy McCall all about you."

Ruby just bet she did. No doubt telling him how her own father didn't want her when her mother died. Relating the number of times she had had to be placed because no foster family wanted her for very long . . . simply claiming she was too . . . strange. More often than not, they just gave her back because she scared them with her "odd ways."

"I'm sure it was an interesting conversation. Sorry I missed it."

"Ms. Deveraux, where have you been all this time?"

"I got into a bit of trouble when I went looking for Amy and Emily."

"What kind of trouble?"

Ruby wet her lips. Fabricating a story that couldn't be verified with authorities in Istanbul could get tricky.

"She was abducted."

All eyes swung to gawk at the new arrival. Ruby scowled at Sebastian. He smiled at her in a way that indicated he knew she didn't want him here. Knew and didn't care.

"Who are you?" Rosemary demanded.

"You could call me a retrieval expert."

"Retrieval expert?"

"Yes. Private contractor. I retrieve people who get themselves into trouble."

Apparently the detective found this plausible. He started scribbling notes. "Who hired you?"

"Friends of the family," Sebastian lied smoothly.

Rosemary snorted. "Ruby's family wouldn't care enough—"

"Apparently they do," Sebastian cut in, his eyes glinting, daring her to contradict.

With narrowed eyes, Rosemary swung her attention back on Ruby, her curiosity clearly piqued. "What *did* happen to you over there?"

Ruby read the woman carefully, gauging her suspicion . . . and buried beneath it all—*fear*. Not of Ruby. But her fear over having lost two girls who had been in her charge. Her fear of having to account to her supervisor when he returned from dealing with the authorities in Turkey.

"It doesn't matter. I'm safe now." Ruby shrugged. "The girls, however . . ."

She looked at Sebastian.

He arched a brow, a warning glint in his dark eyes.

She wanted to confess, to tell the truth, to give Amy a voice against the injustice of her death. She deserved it. Emily, too. They deserved to be remembered.

Instead, she heard herself saying, "I never found them."

Because the truth would get her tossed inside a padded room.

Deputy McCall nodded. "Not surprising. The police in Istanbul have no leads." Her eyes burned. No. They wouldn't.

He continued, "Probably got in over their heads. It's a shame but I've seen it happen with girls like them all the time."

Girls like them. Forgotten. Discarded. Unwanted. Girls like Ruby.

The deputy turned to the door. "Thank you for your time. Glad you made it home safely, Ms. Deveraux. At least there's one happy ending in all this."

Happy ending. Ruby almost laughed. Or wept. She couldn't differentiate from the thick emotion rising in her throat.

"That's it? You're finished with her?" Rosemary danced around him like an anxious puppy.

"I'll write a report."

"That doesn't help. We still don't know a thing about Amy and Emily."

"And why do you suddenly care so much?" Ruby bit out, unable to stop. "You never gave a damn about them before. What's the matter? You might actually be held accountable for the lives of girls you were charged with? Won't that be a nice change?"

Rosemary swung around, the full blast of her anger slamming into Ruby. The intensity of it made her take a sudden step back. "Don't act so self-righteous with me, Ruby! You know what happened over there. I know you do. You could never lie worth a damn." She wagged a finger. "You had a hand in it, don't I know it! You've been nothing but trouble and grief to everyone you've ever met. I was a damn fool to let you go on that trip with us—"

"Enough," Ruby announced, her voice ringing with more strength than she had ever used before.

Maybe it was this new self, the beast in her, but she didn't feel like putting up with Rosemary. Not anymore. Not in her own home. Not with Sebastian watching. Listening. "Get out of my house."

"No wonder your kin washed their hands of you and wouldn't take you in after your momma died." Rosemary flounced out the door, quivering with a hatred for Ruby that felt like noxious gas on the air.

Slapping his hat back on his head, the deputy departed with a tight, apologetic smile. She listened to their steps on the porch for some moments before flicking an embarrassed glance to Sebastian. She didn't want him to know that she had been rejected by her family, dumped into foster care because they couldn't cope with her. That no one wanted her. Not her father. Not her grandmother. Not her two aunts or the myriad of cousins enough to populate various parishes of Louisiana. None would claim her. Her mother's oddball daughter. An anomaly. Something to be reviled. Abandoned to the care of the state.

All she had ever had was this house, waiting for her when she turned eighteen. And she wasn't leaving it. No way in hell was she headed back to Turkey. No matter what he said.

Rubbing her arms, she headed past Sebastian for the kitchen, forcing her mind to other matters. Like making a living. Lord knew no one else was going to take care of her. "I have cinnamon rolls to bake."

This morning, she had notified the Morning Star Café that she was taking orders again. They had put in their usual request for fresh bread. And Ernie's diner wanted their pies and cakes, too.

"Ruby—"

"I have to get back to making a living," she said, stopping him before he offered up any kind words. Sympathy from him would only make her feel worse—a freak in need of pity. She couldn't bear that. Not from him.

He grasped her by both arms and forced her around to face him. "Stop pretending you're so tough."

"What do you want?" She lifted her chin. "Tears? I'm okay. I've dealt with a lot of shit in my life. What she said doesn't even register on my Richter scale."

With a small shake of his head, he dropped his hands. "Okay. I guess you're not pretending, then."

"I'm not. Now unless you want to roll dough for me, step aside. I have a lot to do." Turning, she stepped inside the familiar kitchen where she had baked countless pies and bread. King cakes for Mardi Gras. Hundreds of casseroles for the area nursing home and rotary club. The familiarity warmed the chilled corner of her heart. If she closed her eyes, she could still smell her mother's spaghetti sauce simmering on the stove, hear her humming as she crushed garlic and fresh basil together in her pestle.

"So where's this dough?" he asked, close behind her.

Ruby jumped a little and whipped around. Sebastian stood so close her breasts brushed his chest. With an indrawn breath, she took a quick step back. "W-what?"

He shrugged. "We've got a week to kill before moonrise. Gotta do something while I'm here."

Nodding, Ruby headed toward her old yellow refrigerator. "Wash your hands," she murmured, trying not to let his being here, so near her, in her kitchen, helping her, thaw her resolve in any way. She had nothing left with him. He would soon learn that she could cope with this lycan thing as she did with everything else in her life. She would cope. Without him. He'd see that. See she didn't need him and then he'd be gone.

As she scooped flour into a large glass bowl, letting her fingers trail through the cool white powder, she wondered why the usual calm and comfort did not wash over her in the act.

Instead, her nerves stretched uncomfortably tight. She felt him watching her, just behind her—waiting for instructions, she supposed. His warm breath fanned her neck, and her breath caught in her constricting throat. Her nipples grew taut and aching, straining against her blouse, craving him . . . his touch, his mouth. She palmed a breast, hoping to assuage the hard tip, make it go away. The act only made her burn hotter, the ache intensify. The core of her clenched. Moisture dampened her panties.

He brushed against her. A hard bulge nudged at her ass. She bit her lip to stop a moan from escaping.

"Will you get the eggs from the fridge?" she asked in a strangled voice, grateful when he moved away.

She swallowed a ragged breath, focusing on stamping her desire, on blocking him. She concentrated, fighting the heat behind his gaze. The hot steady flow of desire he emitted that licked fire at her will told her exactly how he would like to spend the remainder of his time with her. And it wasn't in the kitchen.

A whimper tugged at the back of her throat. She felt his dark arousal. It only increased her craving for him. *Damn. Damn. Damn.* How could she fight this? Him?

Her belly tightened and her breath came a little faster. Turning from her bowl, she found him directly behind her again, a carton of eggs in his hand.

His eyes drilled into her, dark relentless chips of obsidian, that strange white light dancing in the centers. A single step was all it took. She flattened herself against the hard wall of his chest, pressing her aching breasts into him.

He dropped the carton of eggs, his arms going around her, clutching her in a savage hold. She slid one hand through his short-cropped hair, yanking his head down with a growl.

Hard fingers dug into her hips as their mouths met, open and eager, tongues thrusting, licking, tasting one another. Voracious beasts coming together in desperate hunger.

They had this. For now, it was enough. She wouldn't think about tomorrow.

22

Ruby led Sebastian from the swinging doors of Ernie's back kitchen, after having dropped off the pies and cakes she'd made that afternoon—with Sebastian's help, of course.

The last few days she had spent cooking and baking, catching up on her orders for the local eateries. Oh, and having sex. Lots of sex. Sweaty, panting sex.

She had discovered multiple orgasms could be achieved in the time it took to bake a pecan pie. She didn't know who was more driven, more insatiable— her or Sebastian. Their lust for each other showed no signs of abating. They no longer discussed the future. And yet it was there just the same. A thick mist from which they could not escape, surrounding them in a tangible fog neither dared acknowledge. They knew it approached. Why discuss it?

Eight o'clock, and Ernie's dinner crowd packed the old diner. Sebastian held her hand as they moved between tables, his strong fingers locked with hers. A sweet sensation. She couldn't remember holding another man's hand. Never remembered wanting to. The contact would have frightened her. Who knew what she might feel? With Sebastian she felt only desire, a steady pouring of warmth from his hand through her. Into her. The same thing she had felt all week.

"Smells good," Sebastian commented.

"That would be the chicken-fried steak. Everyone comes here for it. It's Ernie's specialty." She winked. "Nothing says home cooking like buttermilk, flour and a deep fryer." She motioned to a table. "Want to eat—"

The words died in her throat when she spotted the family sitting in a nearby booth. The perfect family of four. Father, mother, two sons. "Let's go."

"What?"

Dropping his hand, she moved to the front door. Practically ran.

Sebastian clamped a hand on her arm, that hunter look about him again. He looked at her, then swept the room as if looking for a threat he had missed. "What? What is it?"

"Nothing." Her breath tightened in her chest as, one by one, the family stood to leave. They hadn't noticed her yet. But they would. *He* would. She'd seen him over the years. In a town the size of Beau Rivage, how could she not? But she had always pretended not to see him . . . and allowed him to do the same. Even when their eyes locked. Even when aversion washed over him, swiping its claw at her, she pretended not to feel. Not to know.

Sebastian followed her gaze to the gray-haired man with the same brown eyes she had once possessed. Sebastian tensed, and she picked up on his awareness. Understanding passed through him the moment he focused on her father's face.

"That's your father?"

She nodded.

"He lives here, too?"

"Never left," she murmured.

"Christ." Sebastian dragged a hand through his hair.

"Let's go," she repeated, ready to run through that door. From the brothers she had never met. From the father who wouldn't have her because she was a freak. *She's weird, Diane. She's a weird kid. And I can't stand to be around her. My own goddamned daughter.*

It wasn't right. *Wasn't fair.* That sole mantra burned

like a locomotive through her head as her sandals slapped across the linoleum.

She was almost to the door when she stopped. Turning, she faced Sebastian. He cocked one dark brow.

"Excuse me," she said, in a voice that held an edge of surprise even to her own ears.

With sure strides, she crossed Ernie's diner and stopped at her father's table.

He looked up from dropping a few dollar bills on the table. Astonishment crossed the lines of his face. Then something else. Emotion emanated from him in a slow trickle. *Fear. Bilious and suffocating.* The same fear she had evoked in him when she was just a child. Some things never change.

"Hi." Her voice rang a bit too loud. Swallowing past the lump in her throat, she looked from her father's bloodless face to his wife—a small woman with frosted blond hair and pale blue eyes. The complete opposite of her mother. Ruby had seen her around town before. She knew that she was a dental hygienist. Her gaze drifted to the boys. Both in high school. The elder was featured in the local paper a lot for football or baseball. The younger one she knew was big into Eagle Scouts.

Ruby held out her hand to her father. He stared at it as if it were a serpent. She moved her hand to his wife. Nothing. Keeping tight control of her smile, she turned to the boys. Troy, the older, accepted it. The grip warm, firm. His hair was a dark brown. Like hers.

"Hi. I'm Ruby." She took a small sip of air. "Your sister." The words felt good, better than anything she had said before.

Her father sputtered. *Outrage. Horror. Helplessness.* His emotions rushed her in a flashing burn. His wife pressed close to his side. "Richard," she hissed. "Do something."

"I know," Troy said. "I've always wanted to meet you."

His mother whipped her head to stare at her son. "You *know?*"

"Uh, yeah. Beau Rivage is a small town, Mom."

Smiling suddenly became easier.

Her younger brother shook her hand now. "Hi, David," she murmured. Remembering Sebastian's presence at her side, she stepped to the side and included him. "This is my friend. Sebastian."

Sebastian shook hands with the boys. Her father and his wife stood several steps behind their sons, not coming forward to greet him either.

"What are you doing?" her father bit out, glaring at her.

"Saying hello." She released a deep breath. "Something I should have done a long time ago." She shrugged. "Why not? We're family, whether you like it or not. Whether *I* like it. I'm done pretending we don't know each other. You *are* my father." She looked at her brothers again. "I'm glad we finally met. Maybe we can sit down for a meal and get to know each other sometime."

Her brothers nodded, murmuring agreement over the appalled sputters of their parents.

Sebastian's hand slid into hers again. For a moment their gazes connected, clung. The emotion she felt from him was different—sweet, tender.

Pride, she realized with a start. A totally new emotion for her. At least when directed at her.

She led him from the restaurant without giving her father a chance to say anything more.

A lightness brimmed inside her. "There's a place out on the highway. Fewer locals. Lots of truckers, but they make a helluva burger."

Behind the wheel of her car, Sebastian smiled. "Let's go. The last thing I want on my hands is a hungry lycan." His smile slipped. And just like that, tension returned, attention called to the very thing they had become so adept at ignoring in the past. "That was stupid," he muttered.

She sighed, turning her attention outside the window, studying the flashing blur of trees.

For a moment, it had been all about her triumph. She had forgotten about that other part of herself. The part she would rather forget.

Ruby's stomach growled the moment they stepped from the car into the cool dusk, the aroma of a charcoal grill and searing meat from the truck stop slamming into her. She could smell it all. The sizzling, succulent beef, the pungent richness of boiling crawfish and andouille sausage.

Her stomach grumbled. "It smells like heaven. I don't think food ever smelled so good."

"You'll get accustomed to it."

She slid him a glance. "Why is that?"

"Your heightened senses."

Again, hating the reminder of what she was, she fell silent as he held open the glass door. They took a booth near a window facing the highway. Cars and trucks rolled past, a steady roar in the distance.

They ordered cheeseburgers with a large side of onion rings. The waitress didn't spare Ruby a glance, her gaze glued on Sebastian and with his gorgeous David Beckham looks. Even walking away, she nearly ran into a bus boy, too busy staring at Sebastian.

"Guess you're used to that."

"What?" He glanced up from rotating a ketchup bottle between his thumbs.

"Women falling over themselves for you."

He snorted. "And you're not used to men fawning over you?"

She angled her head. "You're kidding, right?" She took a sip of iced tea. "I don't exactly have an active social life."

"Well, that's not because you're not attractive."

"Maybe." She shrugged, looking away from his burning gaze, uncomfortable with the subject. She knew she wasn't an easy person to be with . . . everyone who ever entered her life made that clear to her.

Moments later, her gaze returned to him. She studied the hard line of his profile as he gazed out into a black night punctuated with the flash of passing headlights. "You always sit where you can see the door, don't you?"

The waitress arrived with their food. She left after making a fuss arranging Sebastian's plate before him.

"You'll learn to do the same. If you're going to survive." He stared at her with dark intensity. "You're going to need to get colored contact lenses for your eyes. They're a beacon for anyone who knows about us. You're lucky you live in such a remote area."

Lucky. She didn't feel it.

She started to point out to him that Lily didn't wear contacts, but stopped herself just in time. Lily didn't need to disguise herself from the world to survive. She had Luc. "The lycans in Istanbul didn't wear contacts—why not?"

"Some pack lycans do. It just depends how confident they are. How big the pack. Strength rests in numbers. Gunter's pack was fairly large. You won't have a pack to cover you."

No, she didn't have a pack. She didn't have anyone. After pissing off Adele, she wasn't even sure she had her.

"Beau Rivage is pretty much off the radar. If a pack of lycans lived here, our population of forty-five hundred would have noticeably suffered." And she could only assume no lycans meant no hunters were hanging around either. So she didn't have to worry about some agent picking her off coming out of the supermarket.

A pair of motorcycles pulled into the parking lot just then. The riders climbed down, set their kickstands and entered the restaurant with helmets tucked under their arms. They were different from the other patrons. Hard eyes with cruel lips. Those pitiless eyes traveled the room, missing nothing. They landed on Sebastian and Ruby.

And stayed there.

Ruby tore an onion ring between her fingers, her stomach inexplicably knotted.

The pair exchanged glances as they took a table beside their booth, hardly sparing a glance at the menus the waitress brought them, gazes intent on Ruby. She shifted on the booth's seat. Somehow she didn't think it was because she looked cute.

Sebastian arched a brow at her, appearing relaxed and easy with his arm flung behind the back of the booth. Except his eyes told a different story. The light at the center writhed. The muscle in his jaw flickered. Tension simmered in him.

"Why are they staring?"

"Don't you know?" He smiled as if they discussed something light and amusing. A normal couple out to dinner. "Look at them, Ruby. What are they?"

Sipping her tea, she studied them covertly. The hardened features, the eyes like ice. One of them sat with his hand buried in his jacket pocket.

"Hunters," she murmured, quite sure they were human even with their inhuman eyes. Hunters passing through, probably heading their way south to one of the bigger cities—Lafayette, Baton Rouge or New Orleans.

"Yeah. NODEAL agents. So much for Beau Rivage being off radar."

She didn't bother explaining that they only ran

into them because they'd left town for a truck stop on a busy highway. She'd think twice before doing that again.

"What do we do?"

"Finish our food and leave." He finished the last of his burger as if two hunters didn't sit feet away, staring them down like prey.

Ruby played with a crisp onion ring, no longer able to eat.

Finished, Sebastian tossed a couple bills on the table. "Let's go."

Ruby slid from the booth. Sebastian gripped her elbow, guiding her from the restaurant. She didn't need to look over her shoulder. She felt them follow. Felt their adrenaline on the air, pungent as sweat in a locker room.

Her heart accelerated in her chest. Sebastian led them outside, as if he were unaware of the two agents on their heels. At the door of her car, he stopped and turned.

"Evening," he greeted. "Can I help you guys?"

The pair exchanged looks. Both buried their hands deep in their jacket pockets, and she knew they were armed, that she and Sebastian probably stood in the line of fire.

One of them spoke. "We're not after you. Just give her to us and you can walk away."

Clearly they didn't realize Sebastian fell in the nonhuman category, too.

He cocked his head as if considering. "I don't think so."

"Look," the other one bit out. "You don't know what you're dealing with. Do yourself a favor and get in your car and drive away now. While you still can."

"I think it's more accurate to say *you* don't know what you're dealing with. Walk away, forget you ever saw her, and you can live."

They laughed, the sound a low chuckle that grated her nerves. "You should keep better company." Their laughter stopped. "You're a dead man now."

Guns flew free. Her heart seized.

Ruby smelled the burn of silver on the air as bullets exploded from the chamber.

23

Sebastian's hand slammed down hard on her shoulder, shoving her, pushing her clear, but she was already moving, diving to the ground. He didn't need to propel her out of the bullet's path. Instinct took over. A burning will to survive coupled with a keen animal impulse.

With blurring speed, she landed hard and rolled. Gravel crunched beneath her body. The smell of sunbaked dirt filled her nose. In a flash, she popped up in a crouch, fingertips poised, ready to push off the ground and spring.

But she didn't need to.

Sebastian was on the hunters like a pouncing tiger.

She watched as he yanked down on their guns, twisting one weapon around and firing into one of them. The silencer muffled the shot. With a scream, the hunter fell hard to the ground, clutching his thigh, fingers pressed tight over the gushing wound. Her nostrils flared and her mouth salivated at the coppery-sweet scent. She took a step forward.

Sebastian loomed over the one still standing, his voice thick and guttural as he spoke. "You better leave and take your friend with you before I inflict more damage than that." His face shifted then, blurring into the sharp lines and curves of an animal, then flashed back. "The permanent kind."

"Christ!" the hunter cursed, jerking back a step before helping his cohort to his feet. The two staggered away, cursing beneath their breaths and shooting several glances over their shoulders at Sebastian and Ruby.

Legs braced apart, Sebastian stalked after them a few steps, his body radiating menace, hands curling at his sides as if he wanted to go after them.

Ruby watched as one helped the other onto his bike. They revved their engines and disappeared from the parking lot, tires spitting gravel.

Sebastian moved to her side again. "Nice way to dodge a bullet."

"Yeah. You, too." Her voice shook and she swallowed as she glanced around at the still and silent parking lot of the truck stop she and Adele ate at a couple times a month. Her stomach knotted. It would never be like that again, she realized. Her world was changed. She had changed. She had thought, coming home, that she would not have to confront it. She could safely hide. As always.

"C'mon." Sebastian pulled her toward the car. Moments later, they were driving, heading toward the back parish road that led to her house.

She trembled in her seat, her hands twitching in her lap. In a strange way, this was worse than Istanbul. The ugliness had reached her here. Nothing bad was supposed to find her here.

"You okay?

She nodded. "What about those hunters?"

"They'll be fine."

She shot him an annoyed glance. "I know . . . but . . ." She waved a hand. "You let them go. Will they come back?" Invade her world?

His lips pulled into a hard line.

"They will," she snapped, an edge of hysteria entering her voice.

"They'll report to their supervisors and NODEAL will likely recon the area, looking for us."

She bounced her head against the headrest. "Great.

Beau Rivage is a small town . . . how hard can it be for them to—"

"Calm down."

"Calm down? That's easy for you to say. You don't live here. You don't have a home, a life here. You'll be gone in a few days and I'll be—"

"You can come with me."

She rubbed her hands over her arms. "No. I can't. I can't go back out there."

"You're no more safe here than out there." He gestured widely with his hand.

"Damn it," she ground out, rolling her head against the headrest. "Why didn't you . . ." her voice faded.

"Kill them?" He cut her a glance.

Callous, but true. She had been thinking that. Desperate, angry, she wished they weren't out there.

She said nothing for a long moment, and then, "They were out to kill us."

"Yes." His hands tightened on the steering wheel.

"Haven't you killed hunters before?"

"For a long time I've hated hunters as much as lycans." His knuckles grew white. "A lycan raped my mother, but hunters killed her . . . tracked her down and assassinated her because she was a Marshan. Even when she was past the point of breeding, too old to give birth to another dovenatu, no longer a threat to them, they shot her down like a dog."

"I didn't know." She lifted a hand to touch him but let it drop back in her lap at the hard coldness of his expression.

"Yeah." His lip curled back from his teeth. "I hate fucking hunters." He swung his gaze to her again. "But I'm tired of killing when it doesn't seem to do any good. There will always be packs. And there will always be hunters."

But he chose not to eliminate a pair of hunters now? She shook her head. When letting them live was a threat to her? When they would just show up and try to kill her again?

She couldn't help herself. Frustration swelled inside her. "Well, you didn't do me any favors."

"We'll get ready for moonrise tomorrow. And when it's over, you'll leave with me. It's the safest thing to do."

Suddenly the control she thought she had claimed for herself since returning home began to slip between her fingers, elusive as water. "Like hell I will." Rational or not, she wouldn't let that happen. The choice would be hers. He wasn't taking it from her.

"Damn it, Ruby." He shot her a frustrated glare. "You can't pretend this will all go away."

"Especially with you alerting the world about me."

With a groan he dragged a hand through his hair.

"Look." He inhaled. "For now, we'll just focus on getting through the next few days."

"Fine." *The next few days.* She dragged a shuddering breath into her lungs. The memory of lycans as she had seen them . . . mauling Amy and Emily . . . made her chest tighten. She knew this had been coming. Despite trying to ignore its approach. Despite pretending it couldn't reach her, couldn't get to her here. It would. It had.

Sighing, she propped an elbow on the door and stared out the window into the dark night. Woods crowded the narrow road. Another car approached and Sebastian hugged his side of the road. Branches scraped her door. The car passed. Dirt and rocks ticked against the side of the car.

The moon followed their vehicle, nearly full, a great glowing eye peering between a latticework of branches. "I'll call Adele."

"Sure she'll still come?"

"One fight doesn't break a friendship." At least not theirs. Ruby needed her. Adele wouldn't let her down. Adele she could rely on. No one else. Not Sebastian. She wouldn't let herself need him.

Sebastian followed one step behind Ruby as she hurried inside the house, staring at her slim back, the rigid set of her narrow shoulders—and cursed beneath his breath.

He rubbed a palm against his nape. Was he trying to sabotage her efforts? Force her to stay with him? Leave with him? Need him no matter what? No matter that she had a plan in place that actually might work. Might make his staying with her totally unnecessary.

His feet thudded up the porch steps.

He should have killed those hunters. He wasn't into mercy. Not when it came to hunters. He would have killed them before. Before Ruby.

Just who am I anymore?

The old Sebastian would have squeezed the trigger without blinking. Instead, he'd let them live. And he was afraid he had let them live so that Ruby would have to leave. With him.

On the porch, he paused. Skin tightening, he turned and faced the night, a sudden awareness settling in his bones.

"Sebastian?" A board groaned. He heard her step away from the front door, the porch creeping imperceptibly beneath her feet as she moved toward him.

"Something's coming." He stared out into the night even though he knew he would see nothing. Nothing was there. Yet.

Her gaze burned into his profile. Wind rustled

through branches, tugging leaves loose. Silvery moonlight drifted through the branches, casting patches of light on the ground. He sniffed the air. It was still there. That faint hint, a whiff . . .

"The hunters from the diner?" Panic fed her voice.

He shook his head, his features tight, itchy as he turned his face into the breeze. "No. They're gone. This is something else. Something . . ."

"What?"

"Something distant."

"Distant? Then how do you even know anything's coming?"

He heard the incredulity in her voice, but he'd spent a lifetime honing his instincts. First, running. With his brother and mother. Always one step ahead of lycans and hunters. Then tracking. Hunting. Always hunting.

Years of hunting. No friends to speak of. No parents. Even his brother he let slip away. All so that he could bury himself in the hunt, the kill. Maybe not the best life, but one that had taught him how to survive . . . how to detect threats when they were only a whisper on the air.

He'd been at the game long enough to know when the tables turned and suddenly *he* became the hunted.

"Let's go inside." Grasping her elbow, he led her into the house. But not before casting one more lingering look over his shoulder. They needed to move. As soon as moonrise ended. He would give her no choice.

In days, they would be gone from here. And far from whatever was coming for them.

24

Ruby paced the floor of her vegetable cellar. The concrete was cracked in several places, leaking moisture from the earth. The air felt cool even without the benefit of air conditioning. In summers past, whenever the AC gave out, she and her mother would fold laundry down here with only each other and the radio for company.

A lone mattress sat on the floor, a blanket tossed over it. For her comfort. She shuddered. It was hard to imagine ever feeling comfortable with what was coming.

Sebastian leaned against the wall, watching her beneath a heavy-lidded gaze as she prowled the cell, waiting for Adele. She couldn't help it . . . her mind drifted to another room about the same size halfway around the world. Her mouth dried. But this time it would be only her down here.

"You'll be okay down here?" Adele called, her feet falling soundly as she descended the wood steps. She carried a pillow and a jug of water with her.

"Sure."

Adele stopped next to her. "Just want to make sure."

"Yeah, well. I don't have a choice." She spoke distractedly, rubbing the side of her face. "Have I told you how much I appreciate and love you for doing this?"

The two of them had patched things up, but Ruby still regretted the harsh words she'd spoken.

Adele brandished the syringe, flicking it once with her finger. A drop of fluid glistened from the tip. It would knock Ruby out within half an hour. At least according to Dwayne's instructions.

She held out her arm and didn't flinch as Adele pushed the needle through her flesh. Not when the alternative—being awake and cognizant during her transition . . . feeling nothing but the blood hunger, the terror of her body becoming something else— was the only other option.

Pressing her arm close to her side, she rubbed the spot of injection. "You should go ahead and leave now."

Adele's eyes glinted wetly. "I'll leave the basement, but not the house. I'm here for you, Ruby." Her nose wrinkled and she winked. "I'll wait it out with lover boy upstairs."

Heat crawled her face and she tossed a nearby pack of toilet paper at her friend. It bounced off Adele's back as she moved up the steps.

"Don't come down here until morning," Ruby reminded sharply.

Adele's feet beat out a steady rhythm. "You've only said that like fifty times."

Sebastian arrived at the top of the stairs, his frame filling the doorway. "I'll see that she doesn't."

Ruby nodded stiffly. He hadn't touched her last night. She had waited, lying in the dark, desperate for him. And he had not lifted a hand toward her. She didn't know what moonrise would bring, but she knew she would survive it. And she would not go with him when he left.

That meant he would be gone in three nights.

An ache throbbed beneath her breastbone. As eager as she was to put moonrise behind her, she was not eager to say goodbye to him. She moved to sit on the mattress. "I expect French toast in the morning," she called to Adele's retreating form.

"If you're making it," Adele shouted from just beyond the stairs. "You know I can't cook."

"I'll cook."

Sebastian lingered at the foot of the stairs. She felt his hesitation, sensed his unease . . .

He shuffled closer, away from the stairs.

"You can't stay," she said, her voice fast. "Go."

He couldn't hold her hand through this. No one could. They weren't the same. Fully shifted, who knew how she would react to him? Sure, he could handle himself against any single lycan—*her*. But she wouldn't put him to the test. She wouldn't put herself to that test.

"You can't be here."

"Ruby." He shook his head. "I can handle whatever comes."

"I'm alone on this. I have to be."

His indecision hovered between them. His compassion. It undid her. She had vowed to do this alone, had vowed to handle it. To keep control of something in her life, of this at least. She couldn't rely on him. Couldn't let herself need him.

"I'm always alone," she added. "That's the way I like it."

Her words seemed to affect him at last. His features hardened. "Of course. I understand exactly." And that's because he did, she realized. They both felt the safest in solitude. Trusting only themselves. Neither would have it any other way.

With a brisk nod and a curt "good luck," he took the steps two at a time.

Then, halfway up the steps, he stopped. Turning, he drove a hard line back down the steps toward her, his mouth pressed into a hard, determined line that made her stomach clench.

Before she realized his intent, he seized her by the shoulders and kissed her long and hard. Just when the kiss began to swing into something else, something that sent licks of heat twisting through her belly, he broke free. Nose to nose, he stared starkly at her for several moments. His ragged breath fogged her bruised lips and she leaned forward for more, another taste.

But then he was gone.

She listened as the door clicked shut and multiple locks fell into place, resounding in the silence of her cellar, echoing in the hollows of her heart. For now, and all the generations to come.

As the sun dipped behind the trees standing guard over the house, Sebastian strode a hard line over the floor, walking from the bookcase to the edge of the living room and back again. Impending night hummed outside. His ears picked up the slightest sounds, detected the life beginning to stir, insects and animals that had lain low all day moving now, ready to prowl free.

Adele sat on the couch, legs curled under her, flipping through a copy of *Food and Wine,* a sweaty bottle of Dixie hanging loosely from her fingers.

Being up *here*—while she was down *there*—didn't feel right. He was here to watch over her, protect her—from herself and others. That's why he'd come after her.

Was that why? Really?

He shoved back the small voice inside his head and listened for the smallest sound from below, even though he knew she wouldn't have shifted yet. It took a high moon before that could happen.

"Pacing the floor isn't going to make the night pass any quicker."

He glanced at the female on the couch. With her ample curves and sultry mane of hair, she would have spiked his interest any day of the week. Before. Before Ruby. Only thoughts of Ruby consumed him now.

He and Ruby had shared a lot in the last month— imprisonment, fear and torture . . . their bodies. He could not claim such closeness to anyone else. He'd gained a certain comfort with her that he shared with no one else. His hand tightened into a fist at his side. She could walk around his head . . . and he didn't mind.

"You care about her." Adele watched him with catlike eyes for a moment, then looked down at the magazine in her lap again, flipping pages. "I think you probably even love her."

He opened his mouth to deny this, but she only cut him off. "Don't lie." Her glossy lips quirked. "I know these things. I'm surprised Ruby hasn't already figured it out, but then I guess her own feelings probably get in the way. She probably thinks what she's feeling from you is just her own heart talking." She laughed hollowly and heaved a sigh. Her gaze drifted over him, her eyes hardening. "But this is new to Ruby. I hope you're not going to break her heart and bail out on her like everyone else in her life. Because if you mess with her, you'll have to answer to me."

He smiled at that. A threat from a mortal woman . . . "Yes, ma'am."

She nodded as if matters were settled. "So how long are you going to hang around up here?" She motioned to the floor with one hand as she flipped another page. "Ruby needs you down there."

He stared at her for a moment, her words sinking in. She was right. What the hell was he doing up here? Ruby was scared. Frightened. No matter what she said. The transition alone would feel like she was being torn inside out. As a boy, those first times had been nothing short of traumatic. Until he learned to embrace it, to stop fighting his body's change. Now he did it with ease, in a blink of the eye. Ruby wouldn't know how to do that.

Even different as they were, he could help her through it. Coach her through the worst. He could handle one lycaness. He was stronger, older, more experienced, not a mortal in danger of moon-driven hunger. And none of that should bother him anyway. Loaded with sedatives, she would sleep through the worst of it. She probably wouldn't even know he was there. But he would. He would know.

He had to go to her.

"What are you waiting for?" Adele asked.

"Absolutely nothing." Turning, he headed toward the kitchen, stopping at the door leading to the cellar that he had added extra locks to—intent on one goal. *Ruby.*

Ruby needed him. It was enough. It was everything.

One hand on a bolt, he jerked to a sudden stop. The hairs on his flesh sprang to chilling awareness, vibrating. Rotating on his heels, he moved, passing back through the living room, past Adele's watchful gaze, pausing before the front door.

A threat approached. Outside. Just beyond the porch. His every nerve buzzed in warning, his skin tightening, stretching. His bones pulled, at once painful and darkly satisfying.

"Adele. Get upstairs. Now. Hide yourself." Even as he instructed this, he knew it wouldn't matter. Whatever coming wasn't human. If the creature defeated him, Adele couldn't hide.

"What—"

"Go!" he barked.

She scrambled from the couch. Her feet thundered up the stairs.

The familiar heat of the beast rose up inside him, preparing to battle whatever advanced as his hand closed around the doorknob, his mouth dry as sandpaper. He couldn't lose. Ruby was just below. Defenseless, sedated.

Growling, he shook his head. How could he have thought he could ever leave her? He would never feel satisfied with the notion of her alone during every moonrise with only Adele, a mortal, to serve as watchdog. How could he have thought that would be okay? Right now, in this moment, with darkness closing in, the moon rising on the night, and a faceless threat drawing closer, she needed him.

And she always would.

He opened the door and stepped out onto the porch. A figure emerged from the trees, his strides slow, deceptively easy, the rolling gait of a predator.

Sebastian marked him instantly: the golden dove-natu from Istanbul. A vengeful light glittered at the centers of his eyes. Apparently he had survived the explosion . . . and was pissed as hell.

"You're alive," Sebastian announced, his voice thick and guttural, teeth gnashing. The words rang with deadly calm—a direct contrast to the wild stretch-ing, turning, tightening of his muscles, readying to battle.

"Yeah." He carried a backpack over one shoulder, but tossed it aside as he squared off in front of Sebas-tian. Wind whispered through the night, lifting the dovenatu's dark blond hair.

In an instant, he shifted, muscles straining, swell-ing against his clothes, his face blurring into feline-like lines. "But you're not."

They sprang for each other, bodies a hiss on the wind. Only one thought churned through Sebastian as he smacked into hard flesh and bone. He had to win. His own fate didn't even register.

If he lost, the bastard would find Ruby and de-stroy her. She needed him. He wouldn't fail.

25

Ruby breathed heavily from where she sprawled on the mattress. Her chest rising and falling with rapid breaths, air sawing from her lips and nose as if she could not draw enough inside her. Heat smoldered through her, flaming her insides raw.

Sitting up, she blinked free of the grogginess in her head and glanced at the digital alarm clock. *Seven P.M.*

Rolling onto her back, she beat a fist against the mattress, arching in agony. She should be unconscious. Dead to the world.

"Damn it, Dwayne." The dosage must have been off. She had to endure this awake and aware.

No light permeated the room, but she didn't need to be outside to know that dusk had fallen. Moonrise was on her.

With a moan, she curled into a tight ball and clutched her twisting belly. Was this how it was supposed to be? Was it supposed to hurt this much? Did she have this to look forward to for the next three nights?

Every month? Every year?

A sob scalded her throat. She flipped to her stomach and buried her mouth in the mattress to muffle her scream as her limbs twisted, tore, grew . . .

One name welled up inside her, exploded from her lips in a voice she didn't even recognize, too thick and garbled to be her own.

"Sebastian!"

Writhing, she strained, bending her spine as her body turned itself inside out.

Worse than the pain, than the unbearable pulling and stretching, was the building hunger. The burn in her blood. The devouring of herself.

Squatting on all fours, she turned her head side to side, inhaling deeply through her nose. Her fingers flexed on the cold cement floor. All at once, the earth became a live, pulsing thing beneath her. The woods surrounding her house were soaked with life that beckoned. Everything reached through the walls, seeking her, calling her awake, urging the hunger on.

Her nostrils flared. A familiar scent reached her—Adele.

She was close. The only human within miles and Ruby zoned in on her. Springing to her feet, she sniffed harder, drawing air into her lungs. She surged forward, breaking through the door as if it were cardboard.

Wood splintered, but she could not stop to care, to worry, to do anything besides follow her nose, her bloodlust.

And hunt down Adele.

"You're good," the dovenatu announced, springing to his feet after Sebastian had just sent him colliding into a tree.

"Not the easy kill you were looking for?" Sebastian taunted.

"I'll kill you soon enough." He shook his arm, which dangled oddly, clearly broken from the impact. Giving it a turn, he set it back in place and began circling Sebastian. "What do I call you?"

"Why does it matter?"

"Occasionally, I like to know the names of those I kill. At least, those I especially enjoy killing."

"And why am I so special?"

A scar ticked white at the corner of his lip. "You took someone very important from me."

Sebastian stilled, his guard slipping. "The bomb?"

"Yeah," he bit, voice sharp as cut glass. "The bomb. You know all about that, don't you?"

"Yes. I do," he responded, understanding at once why this dovenatu had followed him here. This was personal. He wouldn't quit until one of them was dead. "Too bad about that," Sebastian said before launching him an uppercut to the jaw. The hybrid's head snapped back.

Straightening his neck and facing his adversary again, the dovenatu's eyes glittered with black hatred. "She was fifteen years old," he ground out. "For her, you'll die. In great agony." His gaze skipped to the house. "You and the lycan bitch that you've paired up—"

Sebastian struck him. Again and again, determined to kill, destroy, *win*. Whatever it took to protect Ruby.

The dovenatu staggered, falling. Straddling him, Sebastian pounded him into the earth, one hand moving to the silver nitrate-covered blade at his belt.

Pulling it free, he plunged it into his enemy's chest. The bastard slapped his hand around Sebastian's fist, clutching the grip as he fought to push it deeper.

The dovenatu gasped, spittle flying from his lips as the blade wedged itself deeply, striking a rib. Still he fought, clawing Sebastian's hand.

Sebastian clung, knowing he couldn't let go . . . couldn't lose Ruby.

A scream shattered the evening.

He froze, looking wildly from the dovenatu to the house.

"Adele?" he shouted.

Another scream. Then another. Agony filled the sound. Terror.

And then he knew.

"Ruby!" Somehow she'd broken through the door.

Releasing the dovenatu, he ran for the house, forgetting all about the dovenatu out for his blood in his panic to save Adele, to save Ruby from a total descent into darkness. Before he lost her forever.

Ruby inhaled great gulping breaths, fighting against the terrible twisting within her body. Air hissed out between her teeth at the burn consuming her.

Adele screamed, backing as far against the bedroom wall as possible. She held up a hand, feebly, as if that would keep Ruby away. "Ruby! Don't! It's me! *Your friend!*"

Ruby knew that, but the knowledge paled, faded to nothing beside the dark, clawing hunger.

She slid a step closer, her gaze feasting on the pulse hammering against Adele's neck, jumping against the tender skin. Sweet, ripe life. So sweet, so tempting. Too much for her to resist.

In that moment everything else vanished. Everything but her need, her thirst for flesh, for blood.

Adele slid to the floor, her back against the wall, knees rising to her chest. Her colorful skirt pooled around her in a wide fan.

Her whimpers scraped the air, a soft and steady hum that gradually penetrated the fog.

"Ruby . . . no, no." Adele buried her head in her bent knees, fingers white and trembling where they clutched.

Adele's fear washed over her. *Black terror*. It seized Ruby by the throat so tightly she couldn't breathe. Her stomach cramped from the ache of it. Wave on bitter wave . . . a heavier surge even than the demanding hunger.

Stopping hard, she shook herself. And looked down.

She caught sight of her hands . . . fingers that more resembled talons with their long nails. The sight made her wince.

Horror surfaced . . . mingling with Adele's terror.

Not Adele. Not her best friend.

Moaning, she buried her face in her strange, alien hands, willing for the torment to end.

"Ruby?" Adele whispered.

Ruby looked out from her hands, gazing at Adele's tear-streaked cheeks, and felt her friend's fear all over again.

"I can't," she said, her voice thick in her mouth, rough and strange. "I can't hurt you. Please don't be afraid."

Her hunger faded to a dull ache, and realization dawned with blinding clarity.

I can't feed on anyone because their pain will be mine.

The fact struck her with such force that she gasped, dropping her hands. To hurt someone was to hurt herself, bringing their agony down on herself. Even her new lycan instincts wouldn't permit such a thing.

"Ruby?" Adele whispered again.

"I'm okay," she choked, sliding one step nearer.

Adele flinched, her eyes uncertain.

Ruby's stomach cramped at her friend's lingering fear. "Adele, it's me. I'm okay. I'm not going to hurt you."

Adele's expression relaxed, a slow smile spreading over her features as she finally understood. "You can't, can you?"

Ruby shook her head, relief flooding through her, chasing the last of the dark hunger into shadow. Adele's happiness filled her, and it was sweet.

She might be forced to turn every moonrise, but the bloodlust would not rule her. She might be a lycan, but she still possessed free will.

Feet pounded up the stairs.

Then Sebastian was there, in the doorway, his gaze wild. He grabbed hold of Ruby as if he expected her to launch on Adele in a raving fit.

"Sebastian," Adele called, but he wasn't looking at her. His gaze crawled over Ruby with furious intensity as she stood calmly still in his grip, not even resisting the hard hands on her arms.

"Ruby," he breathed, staring at her in wonder. *Awe. Relief.* And something else. Something Ruby had never felt before. "You're not . . ."

A monster. A killer. The thing you've spent a lifetime hunting.

She nodded. "I know. I'm okay."

His gaze continued to drill into her. "Of course." His expression of wonder turned to understanding. His mouth curved into a stunning grin. "You're an empath. You can't kill anyone. Not without suffering, too. Do you know what this means, Ruby? You're saved."

Saved.

And she didn't need him.

She nodded. Sebastian's hands on her arm softened. She glanced down and closed her eyes at the sight of his hand, masculine, strong, *beautiful*.

Her flesh was sinewy, lightly dusted with hair, a grayish-brown next to his tanned hand. The sight was just . . . wrong.

Her fingers drifted up, brushing the strangely taut skin of her face. The monsters she had left behind in Istanbul flashed across her mind. *She was that now*. She shut her eyes tightly against the thought.

"Hey." Sebastian's voice bit out. "Don't. Don't close your eyes." He gave her a hard shake, his anger, determination, sinking into her.

She opened her eyes to look at him.

His gaze settled on her, eyes as dark as slate, the centers glowing white light. "This is you now. Accept it. Live with it. Don't hate it—don't. This does not define you. You're . . ." His voice faded, mouth working. Emotion swelled in him, sweeping over her in a warm, tender caress. It was there again, that indefinable feeling. Something she'd never felt before.

But it felt good.

Before it disappeared.

She gasped, surging in his arms. *Black fury*. It

swamped her like an icy cold douse of water. So cold she hissed from the killing sting. She turned, twisting in Sebastian's grasp, listening to the ominous fall of footsteps, shivering where she stood at whatever drew near. Stalking them with unhurried menace.

"Oh, God! Sebastian. What—"

His fingers tightened on her arm, his body tensing. "He's coming. Get behind me."

26

"So this is where you rushed to." The dovenatu dropped a shoulder against the door, plucking at the bloodied mess of his shirt. "We were in the middle of something."

Sebastian positioned his body in front of Ruby motioning Adele to the corner of the room. Dragging air into his lungs, he released himself, arms stretching out at his sides as he let the beast surge forward.

With a savage smile, the fair-haired hybrid pushed off the door, laughing harshly, the sound cruel and mirthless. His gaze dropped to his ruined shirt. He fingered the shredded hole where the knife had penetrated. "This is the last blood of mine you'll spill." In his eyes, a vast coldness.

His gaze slid to Ruby. "Seems a bit passive for a lycaness."

"She's not like them," Sebastian bit out, his words thick and tangled in his mouth. "Leave her be."

"Lycans are all the same."

"She's not one of them." Sebastian's chest lifted on a heavy breath.

"Not soulless, unholy aberrations?" he mocked.

"And what are you? Don't tell me." Sebastian snorted. "You were amassing an army of lycans for some noble purpose."

"Well, you took care of that, didn't you? Too bad you didn't finish me off. You'll pay for . . ." Something flickered in his gaze, the faintest hint of life, of fire in the depths of cold. "You'll pay for *her*."

In a flash, the hybrid transformed, face blurring as he launched himself at Sebastian.

Ruby's guttural scream filled his head as he crashed through the upstairs window. The dovenatu's body pressed heavily on him. Pain lanced his neck, stunning and intense, as they fell in a shower of glass. Black spots danced before his eyes. Their bodies tore apart as they tumbled down the roof.

Sebastian hit the earth with a teeth-shattering jar. He flung his hand to the spot on his neck where he felt incredible pressure. His fingers met sticky warmth—and a large, jutting piece of glass. With a growl, he pulled it free of his jugular, gurgling at the hot gush of blood.

With one hand pressed to his neck, he struggled to a sitting position even as the blood ran hotly from his body. He needed time to regenerate. More time than he had. Time this bastard wasn't going to give him.

Leaves and dirt crunched. A pair of legs stopped before him, filling his vision.

A soft click echoed on the night, reverberating on the air like the thrum of a wire.

Sebastian looked up, the simple move shooting agony through him.

The dovenatu gripped a shiny silver lighter in one hand. "I gave a great deal of thought about what I would do to you when I found you. The entire flight over here, that is all I thought about." His lips twisted in a savage grin. "I wanted it to be extra-special for you." With a flick of his wrist, he opened the lighter. The tiny blue-orange flame flickered. In his other hand, he clutched a small bottle of lighter fluid. "Figured death in flames would be the most appropriate. Suitable, all things considered."

Grunting, Sebastian shoved to his knees. He pressed harder at his neck, as though that could help, could staunch the flow and restore him.

Facing his enemy, his thoughts drifted to Ruby, emotions a burning rush inside him at the thought of leaving her alone to face this merciless bastard.

Run, Ruby. Get away. He hoped she read him, inferred his emotions correctly. *Hear me, Ruby. Run. Run. Don't make my death have been for nothing. Get away.*

At that moment, a truth asserted itself. Maybe the only thing in his life he ever knew to be true. Absolute and unwavering.

If Ruby lived, he could die.

Her life meant more to him than his own. He'd be okay with dying. His gaze dropped to the twisting blue-gold flame. With ending it like this. *As long as she lived.*

His gaze lifted, stared into the other dovenatu's face, into cool eyes. Vengeance. No mercy there.

Lighter fluid rained down on him in a swaying arc, splattering his jeans, soaking him to the skin. The pungent oil stung his nose, the black odor rising up. Death mingled with the coppery aroma of his own blood. He followed the single spray as it squirted a path over his body, unable to move. To resist. To even run from it.

"She didn't do it," he ground down against his teeth, swaying, trying desperately to stay upright on his knees. "She wasn't involved. Let her go. Leave her be."

"Is that what matters to you right now? Her life?" He cocked his head, eyes glinting a glacial blue.

Sebastian managed one jerky nod.

"Good," he bit out. "After you, I'll finish her. Know that." He drew a ragged breath. "Know my pain as you die."

After you, I'll finish her. The words dug a blade to his heart, greater pain than the wound in his neck. A greater pain than he had ever known. "No!"

He lurched forward in a desperate surge of strength, diving for the dovenatu's legs, hoping to take him down.

The bastard sidestepped him. With a snap of his wrist, he tossed the lighter high in the air. Sebastian twisted his neck to watch as it descended.

A muffled howl reverberated inside him. Slowly, sinking, winding . . . the scream rippled through him.

Dimly, he realized the scream was not his own. But it might have been, for the terror it lodged in his heart.

Ruby.

She charged from the house straight toward him, fully formed, her lithe lines undulating like a lioness in movement beneath her tattered clothes. For the first time in his life, the sight did not strike deep contempt inside him. Because it was Ruby.

Their eyes met, clung. Her pewter gaze wild with terror. For him.

The lighter struck his shoulder and bounced, skidding down his body, sparking, igniting with a sharp hiss, then a deafening roar.

In a swoosh, flames erupted everywhere, engulfing him. Devouring his scream.

Ruby staggered, nearly losing her footing at the sight of the inferno rushing Sebastian in a roaring wind of red and gold.

She forced her legs to work, pushing ahead, over the torment, over the burn, the damned *burn*. Determined to reach him, help him, save him. To push beyond the agony. The searing pain turning him to ash—death and ash if she did not do something.

Blood dripped from her nose in a steady trickle, running thickly into her mouth. Uncaring for herself, she hurtled past the dovenatu. Dropping to the ground, she flung herself over Sebastian, beating him with strange new hands that were not her own, that belonged to some other creature of night and darkness.

"What are you doing?"

She registered the voice, the clipped accents, knew it was the dovenatu . . . the one who lit Sebastian afire.

She should run, fight him . . . something. Something. Anything but ignore him.

Flames surrounded her fingers, rose up, licking her wrists and arms. The smell of smoldering flesh filled her nose . . . and pain filled her body.

She rolled Sebastian side-to-side, whimpering, rubbing out the flames despite the hurt she felt in touching him. So much *hurt*.

"What are you doing?" the voice growled beside her again, mingling with the cock of a gun beside her head. The scent of silver reached her from inside the chamber. Still, she worked over Sebastian, uncaring.

How could she fear for herself when Sebastian was in this much pain?

Words tripped from her in a dizzying spill. "Sebastian . . . don't die, don't die on me. I can't lose you. I can't. I don't want to be alone again!"

"Good God," the dovenatu spat out. The soft click of the hammer lifted from beside her head.

Steam rose beneath her charred palms, heavy and black, choking in her throat, stinging her tear-filled eyes. Sebastian's dark gaze burned into her through the smoke, as scalding as his roasting body, the whites blood-red. She read the message there clearly. *Go. Run. Get away.*

Suddenly, Adele was there, tossing her a blanket.

She wrapped it around him and rolled him harder, rocking him in the ground until she banked the fire and steam wafted above his body. Gasping, she sat back on her heels and hovered over him, her throbbing hands suspended for a moment, taking a moment.

Swallowing, she touched him again. Because she had to. No matter how much more she would feel his agony doing so. She had to. She jerked when she made contact with his flesh, slippery beneath her taloned fingers. Raw. Black-charred. Melted sheets of flesh. Every severed nerve-ending screamed. Shrieked. Raw and blistered.

"Sebastian," she choked.

She felt. Felt everything. *Killing agony*. His heart beat slowed, skipped and sank into a skittery thread. "We'll get you to a hospital."

Crouching protectively beside Sebastian, she tossed the other dovenatu a glare. He stared down at her, his light eyes cool and glittery, as if he were trying to figure something out. As if he was trying to make sense of her. Indecision warred on his features.

Maybe because she realized it might matter, she whispered in her thick, garbled voice, "Please."

It was as if the single word struck him some place deep and buried. Forgotten. He gave a small jerk and blinked. His eyes altered, looked different then.

Less glittery. Calm. His chest lifted on a deep sigh. "Forget this," he muttered so softly she could barely hear him.

Shaking his blond head, he shrugged one shoulder as though they were nothing to him and reholstered his weapon. "A hospital can do nothing for him."

A growl erupted from deep in her chest, the sound emerging with a will of its own. "Thanks to you."

He cocked his head, studying her intently. "He was right about you." His gleaming gaze slid down her blistered arms and hands before flicking to Sebastian's smoking body. "You're different. You both . . ." His voice faded and he shook his head harder.

His face transformed, shifted back into pretty-boy good looks. He turned then, his voice floating on the night as he walked away. "Keep him in bed. Give him nourishment. It's all you can do." At the edge of the trees, he stopped.

"And then what?" she called, straining anxiously over Sebastian's body, staring at the dovenatu's broad back.

His dark blond head cocked to the side, turning slightly as though he would turn around. "Wait." His voice moved on the night, indecipherable if not for her keen hearing. "Take care of him. And wait." He moved then, so swiftly. One moment he was there, the next gone, vanished into the woods.

"Ruby!" Adele's voice jumped beside her. "Are we taking him to the hospital?"

"No." Gingerly, she slid her arms beneath Sebastian and lifted him, pain stabbing her everywhere. Her skin, her new body that both frightened and enticed. The pain worse than any agony she'd ever felt.

And still, beyond that black, killing pain, her heart hurt the most.

27

Sebastian swam through a lightless fog. Cloying, thick. Dark weight bearing him down, taking him . . . killing him. And fire, still. Blood simmered in his veins. He tried to scream. Give voice to a single word, a name. *Ruby.*

Did she get away? Was she safe?

"I'm here. I'm here, Sebastian."

He tried to speak, to demand—*are you all right?*

His lips parted, cracking flesh. Garbled speech. Something cool and wet ran over his lips, slipping inside his mouth. His swollen tongue moved, lapping, desperate for a taste, for the relief of it.

"Don't speak. Drink. Rest. You're going to be all right, Sebastian. You hear me? You're alive."

Ruby. She was here. She was all right. Nothing else mattered.

He let the fog take him.

Ruby pushed the door open with the foot of her shoe and strode inside the room, the edges of the tray clutched tightly in her hands. Sebastian turned from staring out the window, his look of restlessness vanishing at the sight of her. He pushed himself up on the bed.

"More soup today?"

She tsked. "A bisque. Not soup."

Accepting the tray, he set it on his lap. "I'm fine now, you know."

She nodded jerkily, her throat tightening as an image of him consumed in fire flashed across her mind. "You will be. I—"

"No. I *am* fine, Ruby."

She stilled at the firmness of his voice. Sighing, she sank to the edge of the bed, toying with the comforter's edge. It had been a week since she carried him into this room, a smoking corpse in her arms. He'd regenerated. His skin, as well as the deep wound in his throat, healed in a matter of days. Still, she insisted he stay in bed, unable to face the fact that once he healed, this was over. *They* were over. As long as he stayed in bed, she kept some control.

"I appreciate all you've done this last week, Ruby," he began, lips twisting. "Guess you've proven you can take care of yourself. Look at me. You took care of me." His expression grew grave. "But I'm done playing sick."

She offered a weak smile, teasing, trying to pretend she didn't understand where this was going. "So you mean you want to take your soup downstairs."

His gaze held hers, and she felt something wither inside her at the look in his eyes. "I'm healed."

Sebastian sucked in a breath, bracing himself after uttering those words. Words that needed to be said. He'd played the invalid long enough to appease her. Appease himself. He recovered days ago. He couldn't keep the game up any longer. He was healed. And Ruby was fine. Safe. No threat to the world or herself. Her gift would protect her. Her gift. Not him.

Staring into her wide eyes, into those pools of pewter that did not spell death, he added, "It's time for me to go."

"Go?" she echoed.

"Yeah. No reason for me to stay." He tried to say this matter-of-factly. With no question. He wasn't asking, begging, for her to give him a reason. He could get on alone. Even if staring at her, his heart rising to his throat, he wondered if he could. If he could ever go back to the way he was before, adrift in life . . . and be okay with it.

"You were right, Ruby." He never thought the words would be so hard to get past his lips. "You don't need me. You can pretty much live your life as you always have." He shrugged one shoulder. "You'll shift every moonrise, but you won't hurt anyone."

She nodded. "That's right. I won't." Looking down at him, she asked, "When are you going?"

"Today." He glanced to the window, sunlight streaming inside, urging him to move, act. "It's early yet. I can catch a flight out of Lafayette."

"You want me to drive—"

"I'll call a car."

She nodded. "That's easy, then."

Easy. It was. She didn't need him and he didn't need her.

She glanced down at his tray. "No soup, then?"

"Bisque," he corrected, a smile playing on his lips.

"It's just soup. No big deal," she replied, gathering the tray, her movements stiff, her heart aching. "I shouldn't have made it out to be something more."

He thought he heard something in those words. Something other than talk of soup. He stared hard at her profile, but she didn't look at him. "I'm glad you're well, Sebastian. I—I didn't think you ever would be, after . . ."

"We're resilient creatures. I'm just lucky that that dovenatu didn't finish me." He had tried to understand what changed the hybrid's mind, but could recall little more than the agony of those moments. And Ruby. His sweet savior.

He watched as she left the room, focusing on her slender back, the darkly shining hair that swayed as she walked.

He resisted calling her back. That was weakness. She didn't need him. Didn't want him. Otherwise, she would have said so. Ever since he had shown up, she had demanded her independence, her solitude— her freedom from him. And he had stayed anyway. Insisted on staying because she needed him.

Now that excuse no longer flew. And he had to leave.

While he still could.

"Your car is here." The words stuck in her throat as she looked from the window. Swallowing back the dryness in her throat, she wished she'd brought her tea glass with her from the kitchen.

Adele arched a reddish brow at her as Sebastian's feet beat a steady tempo down the stairs. Ruby dragged a deep breath. He probably heard Ruby's heart beating like a sledgehammer in her chest. Adele's glossy red lips moved, mouthing the words, *Do something*.

She cocked her head and glared at Adele in warning before facing Sebastian. There was nothing to *do*. He was leaving. Naturally. Like she knew he always would.

Sebastian stopped at the base of the stairs, a gorgeous sight in a black T-shirt and jeans, his short dark hair so soft-looking she longed to run her fingers through it, feel it against her palm. One last time.

"I hate to say it, Sebastian, but I'll miss you," Adele announced, adding with her usual candor, "I didn't trust you at first." Her gaze skittered to Ruby. "But I guess you grew on me."

Sebastian grinned. "Thanks, Adele." His smile slipped, his eyes growing serious. "I'm glad Ruby has you."

"You bet she does." Adele looped an arm around Ruby's shoulders. "Sure you don't want to stay?"

Ruby drove her elbow into her friend's ribs.

"Ow!"

"Why don't you go into the kitchen and check on my tartlets in the oven?"

With a sigh, Adele sashayed into the kitchen. Ruby stared after her, wishing she'd never called to tell her

Sebastian was leaving. Adele had shown up on her doorstep, insisting that she needed to *see* him leave for herself. As if she somehow doubted it happening.

The doorbell rang.

"Your car is here." The driver's footsteps receded on the porch. "Guess you need to get going."

"Yeah." He slung his bag over his shoulder.

"Are you sure you're well enough—"

"Ruby. I'm fine."

She gave a jerky nod and moved toward the door. Holding it open, she faced him, determined to feel nothing . . . not the panic rising inside her at never seeing him again. Not anything *he* might feel over leaving her. If he felt anything. That would be the worst of it. To learn that he felt nothing.

Carefully keeping her guard in place, she lifted her chin. "Thank you, Sebastian. For everything. What you did for me . . ." She swallowed. How could she put it into words? "I doubt I'd still be alive without you."

"Yeah." His mouth twisted. "I think you would. As you've said from the start, you don't need me."

But I want you.

His deep voice continued, "You can take care of yourself." Something lurked in his dark gaze . . . the faintest question. Hope?

She nodded, face hot. Did she want him? Yeah.

Sure, she did. He was her first lover. A shudder racked her. *And there would be no one else.* "I can. I'll be safe."

"Good." His lips formed a single hard line. "That's all I ever wanted for you."

She shifted one foot, as though to step forward and hug him. Catching herself, she stopped. Better not touch him. And a chaste farewell hug? As if they were mere acquaintances? No way. She couldn't bear it.

"Goodbye, Ruby."

"Bye, Sebastian." He moved away then.

She watched, chest unbearably tight.

His back to her, he paused beneath the threshold.

She held her breath, not letting it go. Never dropping her barriers. Never letting herself feel. Herself or him.

Just go, Sebastian. Go before I make a fool of myself and beg you to stay.

With a curse, he whirled around and hauled her against him. A cry escaped her. Molded chest to chest, his mouth burned against her lips, devouring her in a kiss that was meant to last. Forever.

Then it was over. He was gone.

On shaking knees, she watched him stride to the waiting car in a long-legged stride. Without glancing back, he climbed into the back seat. She clutched the edge of the door so hard her nail splintered. Behind the tinted windows, he was a shadow. Impossible to see, to know if he even looked at her, staring after her like she stared after him.

Raspy breath fell from her lips as she closed the door, closed herself. Locked herself away where she couldn't feel anything at all.

Adele emerged from the kitchen, her expression questioning. She glanced to the door, then gave a small shake of her head. "You actually let him go? I didn't think you would, actually. Didn't think you could."

"He wasn't mine to keep, Adele," she snapped. "Besides, he wanted to go—"

"How do you know that?"

"Because he left!" Her voice vibrated with hot emotion. He left. Like they all did. Her father. Even her mother. It was just too hard to love her.

Adele was silent a moment before saying, "Did you ask him to stay?"

She crossed her arms tightly over her chest. "I don't want him to stay."

"Yeah." She snorted. "Right."

"My life is fine. Almost like it was before I ever left on that awful trip—"

"And that's a good thing? You want it that way? That *awful* trip finally woke you up, shook you from your cocoon. Found you someone who loves you, if you would just see it. How many men suffer what he did for a woman they *don't* love?"

"He's an honorable man."

"This is such shit." Adele grabbed her handbag from the bench near the door. "I need to go. I've got a date. Unlike you, I want Mr. Right to walk into my life. And when he does, I won't let him walk out." One hand on the doorknob, Adele hesitated, and tossed her a sad smile. "Call you tomorrow."

"I'll be here."

"Of course you will." The door shut with a reverberating thud.

She shifted and rubbed her nose. What did Adele know? She was wrong. Ruby didn't need anyone. She made certain of that. Made certain she was strong enough to manage on her own.

She had her home. Work she enjoyed. She didn't need anything else. Or anyone. And for one moment, as her legs moved in angry strides through the living room, she almost believed that.

28

From the car window, Sebastian watched as Ruby disappeared back inside the house. His gut in knots, he turned and gazed blindly at the back of the front seat. Soon, tall pines whipped past . . . and he wondered, marveled at what the hell he was doing leaving such a huge part of himself behind in that house.

He leaned with the car as the road curved, fingers tapping his knee anxiously. Returning to his old life . . . but who was he kidding? It wasn't something he wanted anymore. Not without Ruby.

He loved the woman—the *lycaness*. Maybe she didn't feel the same about him, but he could at least tell her, convince her she loved him, too. That they belonged together. Maybe more than any two souls did. Once, he would have said they were both aberrations of mankind, creatures that should never have come into existence. All his life he hated what he was . . . because his mother had taught him he should. Then Ruby happened. Even if against his will, she had become something he always hated. Even more than himself.

And he loved her.

The very thing he spent a lifetime hating and hunting and killing. If he could love her, then maybe he wasn't something to be held in contempt either. Ruby deserved love, happiness and all that life offered. Didn't he deserve the same, too? Didn't he deserve her?

Dragging a hand over his face, he bit out in a hard voice, "Driver, stop. Stop the car."

Ruby paused, the flat of her hand resting on the kitchen's swinging door, exerting only the slightest pressure as the panic set in, rising high in her throat, suffocatingly thick as it dawned in her that Sebastian had left. Was gone. Forever.

She didn't need him.

But she wanted him. Oh, God.

She may not need him, but she wanted him. Loved him. Loved him. *Loved him.*

She had been too scared to find out whether he

could love her. Whether he would walk away like everyone else, preferring another life—*any* other life—to one with her.

Her eyes jammed tight in a fierce blink, the tears burning, spilling through, hot liquid on her cheeks. She opened them to a blurred world. A world that she had never seen so clearly before.

She wanted him.

Before she could stop to think, before she let stubbornness and fear stop her, she moved. Spinning around, she rushed to the door. Yanking it open, she staggered onto the porch with a hoarse cry. Leaves scuttled across the lonely yard. Legs suddenly weak, she clutched a porch post, staring ahead, seeing nothing. Seeing everything.

My God, what did I do?

Her fingers flexed weakly over the post as she looked out at the empty space. He was gone.

She let him go.

More hot tears slid down her cheeks. A sob scalded the back of her throat. *Idiot.* She didn't have any way of knowing where he went. She couldn't find him. Couldn't tell him what she just figured out.

She loved him.

Wind whispered through the trees, rustling the tall tops, and she felt it move through her, a cold, lonely wind that chilled her from the inside out.

Unless she somehow found Sebastian.

She started to turn back inside, desperate thoughts churning through her on how to find him. To track him down. The back of her neck prickled. Rubbing a hand against her nape, she turned and faced the empty yard again, her gaze fixed on the drive . . . at whatever she sensed coming down the long stretch of dirt road.

She tensed, thinking of her last unexpected guest. No longer afraid to use her abilities, old or new, she cleared her head, and opened herself to it.

It struck her in a warm rush, sweeping up her chest, coiling tighter and tighter; an emotion she had felt only one other time—at a wedding she catered years ago.

Standing in the back, she had watched as the groom lifted the bride's veil. Nerve or curiosity got the better of her and she spied inside his soul. She had felt *this* same emotion then. *Peace. Deeply sublime love.*

A figure emerged, clearing the trees, late afternoon sun glinting off his dark hair. A duffel bag hung over one shoulder.

He stopped, his gaze finding her on the porch. They stared at each other, devouring with their eyes.

Her lungs seized, a single breathless word—a name—escaping her lips. "Sebastian!"

She was off the porch running. He met her halfway. Dropping his bag, he caught her up in his arms.

Between kisses, they spoke.

"You came back," she gasped.

"I never should have left." He seized her head with both hands, gazing into her eyes and forcing her still. "You were mine the moment you joined me in that dungeon. I don't care if you need me or not. I need you. I'm staying. Forever."

She tried to nod, but he held her too tight. "You're right. I don't need you," she agreed. "But I want you. I love you. I do. I do . . ."

A smile split his face. "Thank God you said that. I love you, too."

"I know," she choked, feeling every bit of the love in his heart, sensing their future through him right then. Side by side. Long and happy and together. "I know."

He shook his head, still smiling as he brought his lips back down to hers. "Of course you do."

TAKE PASSION
to a
NEW REALM.